Murder & Matchmaking

MURDER & MATCHMAKING

Debbie Cowens

Paper Road Press
paperroadpress.co.nz

Text copyright © Debbie Cowens 2015
First published 2015

Paperback: 978-0-473-31569-6
Epub: 978-0-473-31570-2
Mobi: 978-0-473-31571-9
PDF: 978-0-473-31572-6

This book is copyright. Apart from any fair dealing for the purpose of private study, research, criticism or review, as permitted under the Copyright Act, no part may be reproduced by any process without the permission of the publisher. Debbie Cowens has asserted her moral rights. A catalogue record for this book is available from the National Library of New Zealand.

Cover art by and © Henry Christian-Slane
henrychristianslane.com
Design © Marie Hodgkinson, Paper Road Press Ltd.

Printed by Createspace.

Also by Debbie Cowens:
Mansfield with Monsters (2012)
Steam Pressed Shorts (2012)
At the Bay of Cthulhu (2013)

Contents

1	*1*
2	*11*
3	*27*
4	*36*
5	*45*
6	*51*
7	*66*
8	*81*
9	*100*
10	*114*
11	*123*
12	*132*
13	*141*
14	*152*
15	*162*
16	*176*
Epilogue	*203*

1

It is a truth universally acknowledged, that a pug in possession of good appetite must be in want of a biscuit.

This truth was so well fixed in the mind of Lydia the pug that she considered the shortbread, which Mr Bennet held loosely in his right hand, her rightful property.

'Mrs Bennet!' Mr Bennet looked up from his book and addressed his wife in alarmed astonishment. 'That pug of yours has stolen my biscuit again, and I feel it is only right to inform you I have every suspicion that the animal has designs upon the tea tray. It has been eyeing the cakes in a singularly covetous fashion—'

'Fie, such nonsense. Designs upon the tea tray? How can you accuse poor little Lydia of such things?' Mrs Bennet set aside her needlework and bent to lift the pug onto her lap. She gazed at her dog's wide-set brown eyes, glossy coat and dainty features. 'I will not have you speak ill of my Lydia, Mr Bennet. You know that I look upon her as one of the family, and love her just as much as our own four daughters.'

'Considerably more than most of us, I should imagine,' muttered Elizabeth, the second eldest of the daughters in question.

This remark was heard only by her sister, Jane, who suppressed a laugh in between coughs.

Mrs Bennet continued: 'I wager there is not a dog in all of Hertfordshire with a prettier face or sweeter disposition than Lydia.'

Lydia, in evident agreement with this statement, licked her mistress' chin.

Mrs Bennet was a great connoisseur of feminine beauty and indeed it must be owned that she herself was a very handsome woman. As to the sweetness of her temper, there was less compelling evidence; yet in all her forty years she had given none of her family or general acquaintance reason to suppose her a murderess.

At the age of nineteen she had been so fortunate as to win the hand of Mr Bennet, a gentleman of an amiable nature, whose fortune and respectability were greater than she might have hoped to claim. During the course of her marriage, Mrs Bennet had quite unintentionally acquired the burden of four daughters in the pursuit of providing a son and heir to her husband's estate. While she remained adamant that she loved her daughters as much as could be expected of any mother, they were a constant source of anxiety for her as they were all unmarried and most vexatiously unattractive.

Indeed the greater share of maternal affections were

lavished upon her beloved pug, for the dog possessed all the grace, beauty and vivacity that Mrs Bennet's daughters lacked. Lydia repaid Mrs Bennet's preference with exuberant canine devotion and loyalty. When Mrs Bennet found it necessary to embark on her career as a murderess, the pretty pug had faithfully accompanied her. Lydia had scampered at her mistress' side on the riverbank as she grappled with her first victim, Miss Charlotte Lucas, before forcing her into the water and drowning her.

By the time of the second attack, Lydia had developed so strong an understanding of Mrs Bennet's wishes that she charged Miss Fanny Price, the vicar's pretty ward, with such fierce yapping that the wretched girl tripped and fell in the churchyard. Mrs Bennet had then dashed the girl's head with a rock before she had a chance to rise. It had been easy to position the slain girl as though she had fallen against a tombstone, though Lydia had unfortunately erupted into a fit of excited barking as she darted in circles around the body, and Mrs Bennet had been forced to speak in a most severe tone for fear of her raising the alarm.

With her youngest daughter now sixteen, the problem of four unmarried daughters troubled Mrs Bennet more each day. The failure of any of them to catch husbands could not in any fairness be laid at Mrs Bennet's feet. She had done all that could reasonably be expected of a dutiful mother to raise the marriage prospects of her offspring. Nature had not been generous with her daughters when endowing the gifts that could usually be relied upon to attract a husband. Even Mrs Bennet, who perceived her daughters with the generosity of a mother's hopeful eyes, could find little charm or beauty in them. Alas, the poor girls had taken after their father a good deal more than would be advisable for a young lady, especially as he possessed a complexion too inclined to freckle, small grey eyes, and such coarse, plain features as could only be considered tolerable on a gentleman whose appearance was improved by fortune and respectability. Mr Bennet, though never a handsome man, had at least been fortunate enough to have his features softened and improved by years of comfortable living. He could now be considered almost distinguished in appearance, a fate which Mrs Bennet could not anticipate befalling her daughters.

Kitty, her youngest, was an awkward creature of insipid looks and shy stammering. Mary, her next youngest daughter, had crooked teeth and a disposition too bookish and sanctimonious to attract any man. Elizabeth gave her mother the most trouble, with her wilful nature and impertinent opinions. Perhaps her remarks might have been considered witty if she possessed some charm or beauty, but in a girl with such a large, protuberant mouth and sharp eyes, it was most undesirable. Jane, the poor dear, was the eldest and whilst she was prettier than her sisters, she was a congenitally ungraceful girl with a mortifying inaptitude for all accomplishments. Her attempts at dancing were the most appalling sight Mrs Bennet had ever beheld and she compounded this most grievous disadvantage by inclining towards ill health. Indeed Mrs Bennet could not remember a winter that had not been plagued by Jane's persistent cough. Jane had on frequent occasions become so ill as to be confined to her bed, and the apothecary was much sent for – the expense of which might have been better received had the girl not persisted in repeatedly recovering. Was it too much to ask that her daughter settle upon one thing – ill or well, alive or dead – and then resolve to see the matter through to its conclusion?

'Jane, you must take pains to sit up straight,' Mrs Bennet instructed her daughter. 'Your shoulders are by far your best features, but you will never show them to advantage if you slouch so!'

Jane nodded meekly and endeavoured to correct her posture, but the rigid position made the poor girl look even more inelegant and spill her tea down the front of her gown.

'Oh, Jane! You clumsy girl. I declare I do not know what is to become of us all,' Mrs Bennet cried.

She stroked the pug on her lap and wished bitterly that her daughters' hair had some of the silky sheen of Lydia's coat.

'Do not fret so, my dear, all will turn out well.' Mr Bennet did his best to soothe his wife as he turned a page, if only to try to obtain a small measure of the peace he desired. He had often thought that family life might suit him a great deal better if only Mrs Bennet were not always at him to be doing something.

'Indeed, I do not know how you can say such a thing, Mr Bennet. Your four daughters are none of them married, and if not for my best efforts there would be very little hope of any of them ever being so, for you do nothing about the matter,' replied his wife.

If Mrs Bennet regretted anything in life half so much as her daughters' unattractiveness, it was her husband's languid complacency. It was very well for him to avoid worrying about the future, for he would never go without the comforts that money could ensure, but what should happen to the family he would leave behind when he died? The estate, which had been vastly depleted through generations of imprudent profligacy and now comprised little but Longbourn, was to be entailed away to a nephew and the personal fortune Mr Bennet had accumulated would not be enough to adequately support Mrs Bennet, much less four dependent daughters. The only thought that vexed her more than the thought of her daughters being forced to live in miserable squalor was the notion that she might be turned out of her own house to join them.

Such a terrifying prospect would surely drive any sensible mother to murder.

Though she had been surprised to find murder so thoroughly enjoyable, Mrs Bennet did not believe that this reflected any fault or wickedness in her character. She knew she only committed these acts to secure the future well-being of her daughters. Naturally, she would be able to stop killing once her daughters had husbands and there was no further use for such bloodthirsty deeds. Indeed, she felt adamant that she only enjoyed the planning and execution of such matters because her daughters had not been so good as to provide her with wedding preparations to occupy her active mind.

'Though I doubt it will do any good, I feel I must

urge you to do your duty as a neighbour and a father, and call upon the gentlemen come to stay with Sir John at Barton Park as soon as may be,' Mrs Bennet pressed her husband after not more than a minute of peace had passed amongst the family. 'They are both unmarried, Mr Bennet, and quite rich indeed. Mr Darcy's family owns half of Derbyshire and his friend, the eminent physician Mr Bingley, has a fortune of nearly five thousand a year. I will have you know that Mr Lucas called on them yesterday and Mrs Lucas informed me that the gentlemen were very well disposed to meet him, and spoke most eloquently when expressing their condolences over the tragic loss of their daughter.'

Mrs Bennet still enjoyed a close intimacy with Mrs Lucas despite having drowned her pretty daughter, Charlotte, in the river last April, for Mrs Lucas had no knowledge of her involvement and Mrs Bennet saw no need to distance herself from the friendship. She had always enjoyed their ready exchange of neighbourhood gossip and took a great deal of duplicitous delight in consoling the bereaved mother. Indeed, playing the sympathetic shoulder to cry on had quite removed the ill will and jealousy Mrs Bennet had borne her friend. In the afterglow of her victory, she had quite forgiven Mrs Lucas for ever having possessed a beautiful daughter who had captured the attentions of the many eligible officers encamped in Meryton last winter.

'I wonder that they knew of the tragedy at all,' remarked Jane between coughs. 'They can have scarcely been in the neighbourhood for more than a day.'

'I am not surprised that they did,' said Elizabeth. 'I

have followed the career of Mr Sherlock Darcy with great interest. He and his friend have solved many mysteries and have brought some of London's most notorious criminals to justice. The arrival of such a pre-eminent detective in this part of the country must surely be supposed by any reasonable mind to confirm what I have suspected all along: that the deaths of three young ladies of Hertfordshire are by no means co-incidental and there is cause for further investigation. I should not be surprised if Sir John Middleton invited them here for no other purpose.'

'No, indeed, I suppose no such thing,' her mother insisted. She tickled Lydia behind her velvety brown ear. 'Sir John often has distinguished gentlemen come for a shooting party near the end of the season. Detectives, as you call them, may be all very well in London, but I cannot believe so fine a gentleman as Sir John would arrange such tiresome business here.'

'He is the magistrate, Mamma. I do not think it tiresome for him to do his duty and endeavour to see those responsible for such heinous crimes to be brought to justice,' replied Elizabeth.

'His duty to the neighbourhood would be better served if he had not cancelled the Barton Ball last month,' said Mrs Bennet. 'I should think everyone would benefit more from diversion and society than all this talk of death and gloom. I do not know why you insist on presuming your morbid preoccupations upon everyone, Lizzy. You have developed a most unattractive fascination with crime since Miss Charlotte's accident. I have no doubt that these two gentlemen have come to enjoy the many pleasures that only the country can afford.'

'I cannot believe that one of England's foremost minds in criminology would care for such idle pleasures,' argued Elizabeth, for she was never one to be silenced or relent any of her opinions in the face of her mother's admonishments. 'The joys of country walks and shooting, I dare say, would hold little charm to a mind disposed to examine the darkest of human misdeeds and apply itself to the principles of careful observation and logical deduction.'

'Indeed, I have it on good authority that there is some truth in what Elizabeth surmises.' Mr Bennet spoke without looking up from his book, for he did not wish to see his wife's reproachful eyes as he once again took his daughter's part. 'Mr Darcy told me himself that he has much curiosity in the matter of these strange deaths. He asserts that the loss of one young lady in the area might be viewed as an unfortunate event; that two implies carelessness on the part of the inhabitants; but for three young ladies to have died in such short succession indicates something far more sinister.'

'Pray, how were you in a position to have heard the gentleman speak so?' inquired his wife.

'Did I not say? I meant to tell you that I had called at Barton Park this afternoon.'

'You have called on them?' Mrs Bennet was seldom given such cause to smile as to discover that her husband had complied with her wishes.

'Indeed we cannot escape the acquaintance now. The gentlemen expressed a desire to be introduced to you and the girls. They are to call tomorrow if there is no objection or inconvenience to you, my dear.'

'Objection! Inconvenience! How can you talk so? Two single gentlemen who wish to become acquainted with my daughters?' Mrs Bennet laughed in delight, unsettling Lydia, who had been about to commence a nap upon her mistress' lap. 'Why, I would crawl upon my hands and knees over hot coals for such an opportunity! Oh, but there is so much to do. I wish you had told me of this sooner, Mr Bennet, indeed I do. For now I must decide what each of the girls must wear and how to have their hair fixed so that they appear to best advantage when the gentlemen call.' She set the pug down and rushed about the room, ringing for the maid and clapping her hands in excitement. Lydia availed herself of an iced cake as recompense for the interruption.

The girls exchanged anxious looks. They knew their mother would now insist upon commandeering the rest of their evening in preparation for the visit tomorrow. There would be no idle hours for them to read their books, play the pianoforte or pursue any of their own pleasures.

'Hurry, girls, we have not a minute to lose.' Mrs Bennet ordered her four daughters upstairs. 'We must make haste and ensure you are all to bed early tonight, for a good night's rest is essential if your complexions are to be at their best. Heaven knows you girls need whatever beneficial effects sleep may afford your looks!'

2

THE SUN MADE A WELCOME APPEARANCE THE NEXT DAY and while the ivy-covered walls of Longbourn were more suited to gloom than bright sunshine, the hedgerows and well-tended garden appeared very fine indeed in the morning light. That Mrs Bennet's daughters also looked their best was no consequence of any meteorological occurrence, but of their mother's tireless instructions and insistence.

However, it was with a heavy heart that Mrs Bennet reflected that it was still unlikely any of her girls would excite the attentions of the visitors. Such distinguished and wealthy gentlemen must have the acquaintance of many elegant and accomplished ladies in London, and neither man had yet married, though they must have beheld a great many women whose beauty far exceeded that of all her daughters put together. All she could hope was that the Bennet girls' limited charms would be greatly served by there being no other ladies present.

Indeed, had not her purpose in murdering three of the most beautiful young ladies in the neighbourhood been to ensure that her daughters might not suffer from such comparisons?

'Lizzy, pray do not frown so,' Mrs Bennet instructed. 'No, no, you must not grin, Elizabeth, that is infinitely worse. I insist you refrain from any expression that might draw attention to your mouth. And Jane, that cough! Your incessant hacking shall put the gentlemen in mind of a clogged drain. Stop it at once.'

At the sound of horses approaching, Mrs Bennet jostled her daughters into the most flattering positions. 'Here they are, come at last. Are they not handsome?' Mrs Bennet sighed and thought the gentlemen looked very well indeed, but alas the sight of them provoked little reaction in her daughters, although Kitty squinted as she peered at them and bit her lip until Mrs Bennet admonished her with a look. She cast no such baleful gaze at Lydia, who barked and charged about the yard, and then took an aggressive interest in a nearby shrubbery. Mr Bennet, who had been summoned from his study some ten minutes earlier, tugged at his cravat and stepped forward to greet their guests.

'Mr Bingley, Mr Darcy, you are very welcome. May I introduce Mrs Bennet and our four daughters: Jane, Elizabeth, Mary, and my youngest, Catherine.' He waved his hand at the line of Misses Bennet. 'Too many to remember all their names, I dare say, but there you have it.'

'Charmed, I'm sure,' said Bingley, springing forward to shake Mr Bennet's hand.

His companion took a cursory look over the yard, the house front and finally the Bennets themselves, before addressing his host: 'It would be no more to me to remember a mere four names than it would be to perceive that you are lately come from your library, where you had been occupied for the two hours previous; that you suffer from mild hyperopia; and that your left leg, which was injured some time ago, still gives you pain and discomfort in colder weather.'

'I must say that is an extraordinary declaration of facts, Mr Darcy,' acknowledged Mr Bennet. 'I should hardly dare to presume to know myself half so well as you. I suppose I should be flattered that Sir John has furnished you with so detailed a description of my character, although how you came to know of my reading in the library—'

'Sir John informed me of none of the particulars I related, sir. I declared nothing that was not immediately evident from my own observations.'

'You apprehended all that from a moment's glance?' exclaimed Mr Bennet.

'That you have come from your library is obvious from the faint impression in the thenar space, the webbing betwixt thumb and forefinger, and the corresponding mark on the interior knuckle of your forefinger, which are the unmistakable impressions left by hours of reading. That they were still apparent when you offered your hand indicated that your removal from the library was recent, and the creases in your dress confirmed that you had been seated some two hours.'

Mrs Bennet was mortified by this observation

of the injuries done to Mr Bennet's kerseymere coat, and considered it vindication of her belief in the evils of too much reading. She felt it imperative to distract Mr Darcy before he noted the very ill manner in which Mr Bennet's cravat had slipped to one side. 'Perhaps we might now go inside and take refreshment?'

Mr Bennet ignored his wife and examined his hands before placing them together behind his back. 'Well, Mr Darcy, with such an extraordinary talent for insightful observations you must readily have the advantage of everyone you meet.'

'It is not extraordinary, I assure you,' replied Mr Darcy. 'It was as elementary as it is to deduce from the faint mark upon the bridge of your nose that you wear spectacles for reading, and that the hair at your temples has been flattened by the handles – so you wear eyeglasses, not a pince-nez or lorgnette. It is no difficulty of logic to infer that, as you have removed your eyeglasses to come outside, you therefore suffer from hyperopic vision and require them only for reading.'

Mr Bingley clapped his hands. 'Splendid. I can see you are impressed, Mr Bennet. It is a prodigious gift my friend possesses, is it not? I have had the pleasure of witnessing Mr Darcy's incomparable powers of observation for some seven years and I do not think I find it any less remarkable now than I did then.'

Mr Bennet raised an eyebrow. 'It is fortunate, then, that you do not find such perspicacious exhibitions tiresome. I have no doubt you are treated to them with some frequency.'

'Shall we go in? I am certain you gentlemen must

be most desirous to sit down after your ride,' said Mrs Bennet, regretting that her husband had not remained in his library along with his dishevelled attire that Mr Darcy appeared to find so enthralling.

Elizabeth's curiosity demanded one more matter be settled. 'I see perfectly how Mr Darcy observed these first two particulars about my father, but I do not follow how he ascertained that he sustained an injury some years ago. My father's habit of slightly favouring his right leg could be due to any number of circumstances.'

Mrs Bennet glared at her daughter. 'Elizabeth, do not bother Mr Darcy with your questions.'

Mr Darcy cast a disdainful glance over Elizabeth and her mother. 'To the uneducated eye I expect all injuries appear indistinguishable; however, it is not so. The stiffness in the lower leg, the alignment of the foot, the habitual lean to the left and unconscious curvature in the hand, as though one had spent some time reliant upon a cane, are all indicative of a fracture concurrent with damaged ligaments. The most likely cause for such an injury for a country gentleman would be a riding accident where the horse fell and crushed the lower leg.'

'I think we would do better not to trouble Mr Darcy for any more of his observations,' declared Mr Bennet. 'I am sure he has delighted us all long enough.'

Mrs Bennet forced a smile. 'Mr Darcy, Mr Bingley, please allow my Jane to show you into the sitting room.' She nudged her eldest daughter, who curtsied and stifled a cough.

'I have yet to encounter any residence where the arrangement of the rooms was not easily ascertained from numerous and easily observed facts,' Mr Darcy replied. 'The corner room with the northwest-facing windows would serve as a morning room – I ascertained as much as we approached – and the drawing room will be at the back of the hall, no doubt with large windows and access to the gardens, as is usual in country houses of this style.' He crossed the yard in a few long strides and disappeared into Longbourn before anyone could inform him that this was, indeed, the case.

'Lovely place you have, most happily situated,' Mr Bingley said to Mrs Bennet. He held his arm out to Jane. 'Miss Bennet?'

Mr Bingley was such an amiable gentleman that he was one of the few visitors to Longbourn who was not obliged to suppress a reaction of surprise upon entering the house. The exterior of the once great hall had been designed in accordance with the gothic sensibilities of Mr Bennet's wealthy and illustrious ancestor, and it comprised as many looming buttresses and tall windows as the great Sir Clarence Bennet thought a country residence could possess; which is to say a great many more than the architect wished. However, whatever opinion a visitor held regarding the aesthetics of the exterior of Longbourn, it seldom prepared him for what lay inside. Indeed, had Sir Clarence been a more prescient gentleman, he might have set out a provision in his will that his successors preserve the dark and ominous interior decoration and under all circumstances desist from marrying any lady possessed of the notion that Longbourn was in want of a 'woman's touch'. But as Sir Clarence Bennet had not done so, the portrait of his imposing face was doomed to loom over the staircase of a great hall smothered in pink wallpaper, filigreed wainscoting and floral curtains.

Mrs Bennet did not hold high hopes as the conversation continued in the sitting room. The gentlemen were rich, respectable and handsome, which is to say in possession of every desirable quality in a potential husband. Mr Bingley remarked upon the comfort of the sitting room, the warmth of the family home, and the great pleasure he took in the country on a summer's day. Mr Darcy, on the other hand, showed no interest in the Bennets at all and flatly refused to express any opinion on the weather. He wanted only to talk about the deaths of the local girls, as if bludgeonings and drownings were proper topics for discourse in the presence of eligible, if plain, young ladies. Mrs Bennet could not help but resent that a handful of pretty girls, even as corpses, attracted more attention from the gentleman than any of her daughters could merit.

'I understand from Sir John that your daughters were the first to discover the scene of Miss Charlotte Lucas' drowning?' Mr Darcy asked Mr Bennet.

'Indeed, that is correct,' Elizabeth answered, sparing her father the trouble of formulating a response. 'I was walking with Mary and Kitty when we came upon the lake. I expect you are already acquainted with my testimony from the inquest, but I should be happy to elaborate further as the questioning was by no means meticulous.'

'The eldest Miss Bennet was not with you that day?'

'No, indeed, sir.' Mrs Bennet was eager to claim a

part of the conversation. 'Jane is of a delicate constitution and had a cold that prevented her from walking with her sisters that day. It was most disappointing but she suffered it with the greatest forbearance, for she has the sweetest disposition in the world.'

'I trust that Miss Bennet has fully recovered?' Mr Bingley looked most concerned.

'It is a seasonal affliction which regrettably comes and, upon occasion, goes,' Jane informed him, blushing slightly under the gaze of the fair-headed doctor. 'Yet my cough is a steadfast companion, even in the warmer months, as I am sure my poor family could tell you.' Unintentionally, she coughed.

'It is always a burden to have sickness in one's home, a burden most deeply felt by those who carry the illness.' He smiled. 'I am resolved to return here tomorrow with a remedy I have developed that may soothe your cough, if you will permit this humble physician the honour of being of some little service.'

Jane, unaccustomed to such attention and concern, nodded and felt her cheeks burn.

'There, Jane, that's a fine promise for you.' Mrs Bennet could scarcely contain her excitement. 'Your kindness does you much credit, sir, and I wager you could not find a more grateful or deserving recipient for your attentions than dear Jane…'

'I understand that you endeavoured to pull Miss Lucas out of the water?' Mr Darcy spoke before Mrs Bennet might express further effusive gratitude on her daughter's behalf. It was plain that only a minute regard for etiquette and great respect for his friend had delayed his question even this long.

'Indeed, I did, sir. Mary and Kitty went immediately to fetch help, but I could not stand idle and wait.'

'I do not know why you took it upon yourself to wade into the lake like that. Your petticoat was ruined, and your gown – ten inches deep in pond filth – and it was such a pretty print, too.' Mrs Bennet shook her head.

'Because, Mamma, if she had been alive, I might have been able to save her; but alas, it was too late. She had been dead some time, I think.'

Mrs Bennet looked pointedly at her daughter. She had instructed her on many occasions not to use such a frank and unemotional tone. Equanimity, whilst admirable in a gentleman, was not always desirable in young ladies. Indeed it was foolish to throw away the opportunity to display tender feminine sensibilities. 'You must understand my daughter has been obliged to recount the unfortunate day a great many times.'

'Not often enough, I would say, when the culprit has not yet been apprehended!'

'She felt the loss of her dear friend most acutely,' Mrs Bennet continued, as though Elizabeth had not spoken. 'You must not suppose by her matter-of-fact tone that the subject does not grieve her still. I would give anything that my young daughters' delicate hearts could be spared the torment of raking over their memories of that day.'

'In this, we are in agreement,' said Mr Darcy, although his aloof expression conveyed no sympathy. 'I would rather no young lady was ever called upon to bear witness to a crime, much less discover a body.'

'It was indeed a most distressing experience.' Mary spoke up from her seat by Catherine, clasping her copy of Fordyce's Sermons on her lap. It had been her constant companion these last months. 'We have all of us been forced to reflect upon the fragility of our own mortality and prepare for the Lord's judgement.'

Mrs Bennet silenced Mary with a glare, before smiling at Mr Darcy. 'That is very gallant of you, Mr Darcy, to be sure.' Mrs Bennet scooped up Lydia, who had wandered back to her mistress on the completion of her perusal of Mr Bingley's boots. The pug was content that this guest had paid due homage in the form of petting and ear-scratching; she was less certain of the other visitor, who had ignored her.

'Gallantry! I assure you I am guilty of no such affectation. Naturally, it would be preferable for your daughters to have been spared such distress, but I was speaking of my own wishes. Ladies are such unreliable witnesses; young ladies especially so. One never knows what facts they will fix upon and what they will disregard, and as many times as not, they will give you answers they believe you wish to hear rather than what they truly think. I should rather have one man, even if he is hard of hearing or poor of sight, than half a dozen ladies to bear witness to a crime.'

'That does not seem a logical preference at all.' Elizabeth felt the slight of being presumed unreliable most acutely. 'One man might for any number of reasons not have seen all there was to behold. With six ladies there should be a far greater chance of every pertinent detail having been observed by at least one pair of eyes, and with corroboration between them as to the facts, you might be more assured of the accuracy of their accounts.'

'Indeed, that is not the case.' Mr Darcy regarded her with a superior expression. He was a gentleman in possession of the height and inclination to look down on nearly everyone, even when seated. 'Any corroboration between the ladies' accounts would only suggest that they had been given the opportunity to discuss matters. When provided with the chance to talk together they might very well persuade each other that the black horse they saw was actually a grey, that a short gentleman was very tall indeed, and even that it was a sunny day when in truth it had been raining. No, if anything, the account of six ladies is to be trusted even less than that of one.'

'Upon my word, Mr Darcy, you have me quite convinced.' Mrs Bennet chuckled and gave Lydia an affectionate tickle. 'I certainly have the most terrible memory for horses. Ask me about the lace on a dress or a bonnet and you may depend upon it, I shall give you a most accurate account, but I could not rightly do justice to the fine pair of horses you and Mr Bingley rode here this very day!'

'We are fortunate indeed, then, that neither my mother nor any horses were present on the day we found poor Charlotte drowned,' Elizabeth muttered.

Mr Bennet suppressed a chuckle at his daughter's remark. 'I assure you, Mr Darcy, my Lizzy's account is as faithful as any you could wish for. You might very well consider Kitty and Mary as silly and unreliable as any other young girl, I dare say, but do not discount Lizzy. She has a bit more wit than the rest.'

'Oh, Mr Bennet, how can you speak so unfairly of your daughters?' said Mrs Bennet. 'I am sure we would do much better to forget about that unfortunate event entirely. None of the girls' opinions are wanted. Mr Darcy has said as much.'

'I have been oft made aware these last months how little my opinions are wanted,' said Elizabeth. 'When I first spoke of my belief that Charlotte's death had not been accidental, Sir John regarded it as no more than the fanciful notion of a distressed young lady. If Sir John had not immediately dismissed my opinion, if he had understood that it was deduced from sound observation of the facts, some of the later crimes might have been prevented.'

'The gentlemen do not wish to hear your morbid theories. You would have us see murder in every drowning and accidental fall! I blame all those novels…'

Mr Darcy ignored Mrs Bennet and stared at Elizabeth. 'Sound observation, do you call it? There are not half a dozen individuals I consider capable of true observation.'

'You must apprehend a great deal in the notion.'

'Indeed. Observation requires a full and detailed inspection of the material facts, from the microscopic fragments to the physiographic features of the environs, and all this must be perceived without the corrupting influence of bias or emotion. In addition one must add to this a complete knowledge of all scientific disciplines and criminological principles, acuity of all the senses, and a mind greatly improved by extensive reading.'

'I am no longer surprised that you know only six individuals capable of such a task. I rather wonder at you knowing any.'

Mr Darcy regarded Elizabeth with a curious expression. Mrs Bennet could not decide whether Lizzy interested him or displeased him. Either way, surely *something* could be made of the otherwise aloof and supercilious Mr Darcy displaying any reaction at all. He was a handsome gentleman, although his hair was too dark and his features too grave for her tastes, and he was by all accounts very wealthy indeed. Mrs Bennet greatly preferred the fair looks, amiable manners, and kind, trusting nature of Mr Bingley, and it was clear he had taken a liking to Jane from the way his gaze kept returning to her. But what a fine conquest it would be if she could not only outsmart and elude England's greatest detective, but also claim him as a husband for Elizabeth!

'Mr Bingley, Mr Darcy, the day is so fine and the season so fair – would you care for a turn about the gardens? I am sure Jane and Elizabeth would be more than happy to show you all the delights they hold.' Mrs Bennet stood and opened the doors. Lydia immediately darted out, providing an enthusiastic demonstration of the great felicity afforded in running about in circles on the grass and chasing after invisible prey amongst the flowers.

'There is nothing I like better than a walk in a country garden, and I dare say the fresh air might prove most beneficial for Miss Bennet – if she would accompany me?' Mr Bingley stood and offered his arm to Jane.

'I should be delighted, sir,' Jane replied.

Mr Darcy stood, and Elizabeth also rose to her feet.

'Time does not permit for garden walks. Mr Bingley and I have much work to do and must take your leave.' Mr Darcy nodded curtly at his host and hostess.

'Surely, Mr Darcy, you gentlemen can spare a short half hour to enjoy the pleasure of sunshine and good company,' Mrs Bennet said. 'Your friend wishes it, and Elizabeth is a most eager companion, as you see.'

Elizabeth grimaced and wished, not for the first time, that she had had the good fortune to have been borne of a less embarrassing mother. 'Indeed, no. That is, I am sure Mr Darcy has more urgent matters requiring his attention. In any case, I have a sudden headache. Pray excuse me.' She left the room and hurried upstairs.

Mrs Bennet stared after her daughter's hasty departure and noted that Mr Darcy also watched her leave, before he coughed and caught Mr Bingley's eye.

Mr Bingley smiled apologetically at Jane. 'I am sure you will excuse me, Miss Bennet. I am all keenness and should much rather take a turn about your garden – but duty does not permit on this day. My friend is right and we have a great deal of work to do. I shall call again tomorrow.'

'Tomorrow.' Jane nodded. 'Perhaps we might take our walk then?'

'Indeed. Capital suggestion!' Mr Bingley clapped his hands and bowed at his hosts. 'Farewell.'

No sooner had the gentlemen taken their leave from Longbourn than Mrs Bennet proceeded to scold her husband. 'Honestly, Mr Bennet. I am sure you did not say above five words to our guests.'

'One hardly needs to speak to Mr Darcy at all for him to infer every aspect of one's character and habits. Who knows what family secrets he might have uncovered if I had been more loquacious?'

'You may very well take delight in your jokes, Mr Bennet, but why could you not have urged the gentlemen to stay longer? I am sure you could have made them stay.'

'How so, my dear? Mr Darcy seemed most eager to return to his work, and I had no reason to prevent him. Their visit seemed quite long enough to me.'

'You may not feel the loss of their company, but what of your daughters? Jane most particularly wanted to spend more time with the handsome Mr Bingley. Did you not see how he favoured her? And I am convinced that poor Lizzy was devastated when Mr Darcy flatly refused to accompany her for a walk.'

Mr Bennet chuckled and stood up from his chair. 'Did you not hear her talk of a headache? I doubt that Lizzy any more wished to walk about the garden than did Mr Darcy.'

'Headache? Oh, Mr Bennet. You cannot believe such a thing. Was it not perfectly clear that Elizabeth was hurt by Mr Darcy's refusal and made that excuse so that she might leave to conceal her feelings? She is probably upstairs in her room, crying her heart out as we speak.'

'You are an attentive mother, my dear, to so readily see misfortune in such matters, but I can no more imagine Lizzy crying over the loss of Mr Darcy's company than that pug of yours refusing her dinner.'

'Perhaps I will go to see her.' Jane left the room to seek out her sister.

'A mother's instincts know these things, Mr Bennet. I do believe that Elizabeth admires Mr Darcy enough to fall very much in love with him – or at least, she will do, if she knows what is good for her.'

Mr Bennet caught the eyes of his two youngest daughters. They both wore the same uncertain expression as he did, but they all knew better than to stand between Mrs Bennet and a matchmaking prospect, even when there was no match to be made. Mr Bennet sought sanctuary in his library, Mary in the improving sermons of Fordyce, and Catherine in some very clumsy and unmusical practice on the pianoforte.

Mrs Bennet smiled as Lydia returned from her garden romp, panting from her exertions. Despite its unfortunate beginning, the gentlemen's visit had not been without promise. Mr Bingley had been very kind and attentive to Jane, and Mrs Bennet was certain that with her assistance Jane might well win his heart. Mr Darcy was so severe and his manners so unpleasant that she could not determine what feelings he possessed, but he had clearly noticed Elizabeth and something could be made from that. She would urge Elizabeth to show more regard than she felt for the gentleman. Even if he could not be induced to return her affections, it would distract him from his meddling investigations. Yes, Mrs Bennet considered, her plans were coming along very well indeed.

3

Elizabeth, contrary to her mother's assertions, was not in her bedroom, crying or otherwise. Upon quitting the room she had hurried to obtain the sketches she had made of the scene of Charlotte's murder. Convincing Mr Darcy of the validity and thoroughness of her account had proved impossible in the presence of her interfering mother, but if she were to show him her drawings he was sure to recognise their value as evidence.

Descending the staircase, she beheld through a narrow window the gentlemen standing outside. The window being ajar, she could not avoid overhearing their conversation as they waited for their horses to be fetched from the stables.

'You must understand, Bingley, the purpose of our visit was not to hear any repetition of their testimony about Miss Lucas' death, but rather to gain a picture of the neighbourhood and ascertain which young ladies might be targets. I have every suspicion that our murderer shall strike again.'

'Heaven forefend! Do you believe Miss Bennet and her sisters are in danger?'

'No, I do not believe so. All the victims have been renowned local beauties. The eldest Miss Bennet might be considered pretty enough, I grant you, but, as we have heard, her ill constitution keeps her at home.'

'All the same, I feel I must do my utmost to protect her and keep her safe.'

'I am sure you do, Bingley, but there is no cause to fear for her sisters. They lack the beauty and charms that have most particularly connected the three victims.' Elizabeth could hear the snide tone in Mr Darcy's voice and although she could only see his back, she could picture his dark, haughty eyes sneering at her.

'What of Miss Elizabeth Bennet? She has some most decided opinions on the case, does she not? Should we not fear that the villain will attack her to prevent her from revealing too much?'

'If the murderer wished to silence her, they would have done so before now,' replied Mr Darcy as he prepared to mount his horse. 'Her knowledge places her in no more danger than her appearance.'

'I say, Darcy, that's a little ungallant, even for you. There is nothing unpleasing in her appearance.'

'She is tolerable, I suppose, but not handsome enough to tempt our killer.' Mr Darcy swung on to the saddle and Elizabeth jumped back out of view. 'Bingley, I am in no humour to make flattering remarks about young ladies who are of no consequence to our case. We have a murderer to discover.'

Elizabeth leant forward once more to watch the gentlemen ride away. She was still there, listening to the hoof beats fading in the distance, when Jane came upon her standing at the window.

'Lizzy? How are you feeling? You are not too upset, I hope.'

'Upset? No. I am more determined than ever, dear Jane,' said Elizabeth. 'My resolve increases with every attempt to deride me.' Pressing her drawings to her side, she looped one arm under her sister's and led her up the stairs.

'I have not ever known you to lack resolve, Lizzy, but what have you fixed your mind upon this time?' Jane asked.

'In one encounter, Mr Sherlock Darcy has provoked in me a fierce determination to prove him wrong.' Elizabeth hurried her sister into the room, shutting the door behind them and ushering Jane to sit down on the bed beside her.

'Is it because he asserted that a lady's account could not be relied upon?'

'Partly – but I must own as much dislike of his insults towards me in particular as those he has levelled against all ladies.'

'Mamma insisted that you were upset that he said he would not walk with you. I had not imagined that this slight would have affected you so greatly.'

'No, indeed. That is the one kindness he showed me,' said Elizabeth. 'To be spared his company for a walk in the garden. Imagine the offence he would cause in a full half hour of conversation.'

Jane laughed, which unfortunately induced a successions of coughs. When recovered she asked of her sister: 'But, Lizzy, you must tell me. What did Mr Darcy do that offended you so?'

Elizabeth gave her sister an account of the conversation she had overheard, taking pains to impersonate Mr Darcy's sharp, condescending voice – and to make certain she did not unfairly taint Mr Bingley for his part in the conversation, for her sister's partiality for that gentleman was abundantly clear.

'Oh, Lizzy. It was very wrong of him to speak so. So unkind.' Jane shook her head. 'And he never even intended to question you about Charlotte? I confess I am surprised at that.'

'As was your Mr Bingley.'

'He is not *my* Mr Bingley.'

'I think he may well be soon. When two such kind-hearted people take so strong a liking to one another, there cannot be many obstacles to their mutual affection.' Elizabeth smiled, but it soon faded. 'Unfortunately, I do believe that Mr Darcy was right in one regard.'

'Lizzy, you cannot mean that you agree with what he said about you.'

'No – I refuse to give any consideration to his remarks, so it is impossible to state whether I agree or disagree.' Elizabeth's tone was light but there was an iron-clad resolve beneath it. 'What I mean is that he has found the connection between the victims that I had not. I knew Charlotte and the others to be very different people indeed. Their connections, their characters, their tastes, their pursuits, their situations in life – they were so varied as to puzzle me greatly. But to Mr Darcy, and indeed to the murderer, they were nothing more than three beautiful young ladies.'

'You cannot mean they were murdered simply for being beautiful?'

Elizabeth nodded. 'It is the only explanation.' She went to her table and unlocked the drawer with a key she wore on a silver chain around her neck. She took out a large number of papers and a diary, and placed them on the bed next to Jane. 'You see, Jane, I have considered every other alternative. I have examined and categorised every aspect I could determine about their acquaintance and habits, and occasions where they were all present.'

'I am sure not even Mr Darcy himself could find fault in your investigations,' Jane remarked as she regarded the mountain of papers. She held up a diagram which mapped out every dance partner of the three victims in every ball and assembly over the last year. 'You must have considered every possibility.'

Elizabeth frowned. 'Little good came of it. I was certain I would find some clue, some singular connection between them – a dark secret known to all of them, or a thwarted lover whose advances they had all of them rejected. But I have uncovered nothing of that nature.'

'But is it really to be believed that anyone would be so wicked as to murder not one but three innocent ladies without any reason other than malice? If beauty was indeed their connection, what purpose would it serve to end their lives so viciously?'

'Indeed. Sir John assured me there was no evidence of any unwholesome intent.'

'Lizzy! Surely you did not ask Sir John such a thing?'

'I most certainly did. I should mortify a dozen Sir Johns if it might aid my investigation – but it did not. They were none of them robbed, nor did anyone materially profit from their demise. I must therefore conclude that the murderer struck only out of the most malicious and superficial of motives – an impulsive, violent mania borne of a resentful obsession with beauty.'

'Surely even the most jealous nature could not possibly descend to such vicious brutality?'

'I would much rather it were impossible for such an individual to exist, but I fear it is not so. I have read in one of Bingley's excellent accounts of the superior detective that if you have eliminated all other possibilities, whatever remains, however improbable, must be the truth.' Elizabeth took her sister's hand and squeezed it. 'Jane, do you not see? I believe these killings were of a serial fashion. Whether the murderer acts upon design or spontaneous impulse of the moment, I know not, but I do believe that they act, at least in part, because they take pleasure in the act of killing itself.'

'Could such an evil exist?' Jane whispered. 'And how is it ever to be brought to an end?'

'The killer will not stop until they are found, but you may depend on this: I shall not stop either. Not until they are caught, not until there is justice at last for Charlotte, Fanny, and Emma.'

Jane embraced her sister and when she leaned back Elizabeth saw a tear forming in her eye. 'I believe you shall find justice for all our poor dear friends, Lizzy. I only wish I could be of more assistance to you.'

'You have already helped me immensely, Jane,' said Elizabeth. 'I would be lost indeed if I did not have you to confide in and to hear my thoughts. This investigation is such a tangle of theories and information that I am quite dependent on my dear Jane to help me know my own mind.'

'You are very kind, but I wish I could be of more practical aid. Perhaps if Mr Bingley's elixir helps, I might be able to accompany you on one of your sketching expeditions, or to call upon witnesses?'

Elizabeth recalled Mr Darcy's words. Was Jane's confinement at Longbourn the only thing that kept her safe? 'It would be unpardonable of me to allow you anywhere near me when I am to sketch, for you know I am tiresome in the extreme and tolerate no conversation or distraction when I am drawing,' she said with satirical severity. 'I would rather have you safe and at home so you might recover your health fully. I could not bear to lose you, Jane.'

'Well, I shall do my best, if only to please you, dear sister.' Jane smiled.

'There is one more way in which you could assist me further. If you would tell Mamma that my headache has not yet recovered and I am unable to come down for luncheon.'

'Why, Lizzy? I have never known you to miss a meal. You are not very unwell, I hope.'

'No; it is more a theory than a headache that plagues my mind. I must attend to it or I shall know no peace.'

'A theory?'

'It is only that … if the murderer possessed no motive against their victims and acted out of spontaneous impulse, it casts a different light on how they might have encountered them. We know it was Fanny's habit to visit the graves of her parents every Sunday morning, but what if the murderer happened upon her there by chance rather than by design?'

'Then they must have been in the cemetery for some other reason entirely.'

'Indeed. Perhaps to visit the grave of some departed friend or relative.'

'I confess I do not see how that helps your investigation. Everyone in the area must know someone interred there.'

'Yes, but most people do not visit the cemetery as part of their weekly routine, as Fanny did. It is far more common for people to visit on dates significant to the deceased, such as their birth date, or the day on which they died.'

Jane nodded. 'You intend to survey the dates on the tombstones and see which match the date of Fanny's death?'

'Precisely. You anticipate me well, Jane. It is most unlikely that anything of use shall come of it but in want of any other apparent lead, I must at least try to find something to connect the killer to one of their crimes.'

'Of course you must try. I shall tell Mamma that you have no appetite and desire only the time to clear your head. That much is no falsehood.' Jane rose and went to the door before turning back to her sister. 'Only, Lizzy, promise me you will be careful.'

'I shall, and I will conceal a candlestick in my reticule. If any dare assail me, they shall only have themselves to blame for the very sore head they shall incur,' Elizabeth assured her sister. Jane shook her head and departed, leaving her sister alone to prepare for her excursion.

4

The walk to the churchyard was a picturesque one, through sunny fields and flourishing trees. A small lane passed between the tenant farms on the western border of Longbourn. The once-great estate had formerly encompassed not only the farms, but also the land on which the church and churchyard were situated, and the comfortable vicarage on the far side.

It seemed that there was no one around to partake of the bucolic pleasures but Elizabeth and the birds in the trees. Elizabeth inhaled the grass-scented air, climbed swiftly over stiles, and swung the substantial heft of her reticule as she strode along the dirt path. There was little in her present life that afforded her more pleasure than to be out of doors and walking with unladylike rapidity. Only then might she think over the myriad of facts, theories and reports she had gathered in peace.

At length she came to the dense mass of trees which encircled, and indeed obscured from view, the churchyard walls. The road leading to the church lay at the northern side of the vicarage and there was another, narrower path to the south, but Elizabeth ignored both and strode into the trees. While it was no more than three minutes' walk to the gate along either path, Elizabeth's preference was for an entrance that did not pass directly in view of either the church or the sexton's cottage. The walls around the churchyard were low enough that any climber would have little difficulty vaulting them, particularly as a nearby tree offered a low branch that functioned as a very serviceable step.

As she had hoped, the churchyard was unattended. Mr Hardy, whose duties comprised the care and maintenance of the grounds and headstones, was by no means a punctilious worker. Elizabeth had discovered in the weeks following the attack on Miss Fanny Price that his habits were to rise late to work and finish a good hour before sunset. On any evening, Mr Hardy might more readily be relied upon to possess full knowledge of the persons present at The Pig and Whistle public house than the churchyard.

Elizabeth set to surveying the churchyard, noting the dates and names inscribed on the headstones. She had not completed a full three rows of graves when two figures entered from the far side. The tall gentlemen were immediately recognisable and would have been so even if they had not been wearing the same fine black coats as they had at Longbourn not two hours earlier.

'I say, Miss Elizabeth Bennet.' Mr Bingley lifted his hat and strode over to Elizabeth with a warm eagerness of manner. 'We meet again. It gives me very great pleasure indeed, although I fear we may have intruded on your solitude.'

'Indeed you have, sir, but solitude is a vastly overrated pleasure, is it not?' Elizabeth smiled. 'Those that prize their own company above all others' must surely end up condemned to enjoy too much of it.'

'Yes, I believe you must be right,' he said with a laugh before his face took on a more earnest expression. 'And your sister, Miss Bennet. How is she?'

Elizabeth hid her amusement that an absence of a few short hours had provoked the doctor's concern. 'She is not much changed since this morning, but I can report that she looks forward to your visit tomorrow.'

'Perhaps in view of tomorrow's engagement we might defer conversation till then and attend to matters of far greater import,' said Mr Darcy, ever the dark cloud looming over Mr Bingley's sunny disposition.

'I have no wish to delay you, Mr Darcy,' said Elizabeth. 'I am sure you have much to investigate at the scene of Miss Fanny Price's death. Indeed I am come here myself for a similar purpose.'

Mr Darcy directed his gaze upon Elizabeth. 'A similar purpose?'

She had never heard more scorn and derision poured into three words.

'I shall not wait in an attempt to provoke your curiosity,' said Elizabeth, for she was determined not to be intimidated by the renowned detective. 'We each of us have an impatient disposition, more eager to pursue a pertinent line of inquiry than polite conversation; therefore I shall tell you directly my theory regarding the murder.'

'I beg you not try to theorise upon my character nor my case. Your performance would reflect no credit on you, nor benefit me.'

'How can you ascertain that my thoughts have no merit when you have not done them the credit of listening to them?'

'Surely, Darcy, it would do no harm to listen to what Miss Bennet has to say,' said Mr Bingley. 'After all, she was friends with all the unfortunate victims and it is possible that the young ladies had secrets that might not have been known to others.'

'You are right, my dear Bingley. Pray, Miss Bennet, tell me what you know that relates to this case.'

'As to secrets, Fanny had none, so far as I have been able to discover. It was common enough knowledge among those of us who knew her that she visited her parents' graves every Sunday morn. But if the murderer was unacquainted with her habits, they must have had their own reason for attending the churchyard early that morning, for it is unlikely that they would have spied Fanny on her way here. As you will have seen, the path leading here from the rectory is obscured from the road by the trees.'

'Capital! What a first-rate mind you have, Miss Bennet,' said Mr Bingley. 'I do not think I have ever met a lady with a greater instinct for reasoning.'

'Bingley, you are too easily impressed,' said Darcy. 'The observation about the trees is an obvious one and your theory is by no means complete, Miss Bennet. What motive do you surmise would bring a stranger to a graveyard a full three hours before Mr Fairchild was due to commence his sermon?'

'The most logical surmise is that the murderer was here to visit a grave of their own acquaintance, and wished to come at a time when they might expect to be alone.' Elizabeth returned Mr Darcy's gaze with unflinching boldness. 'If the date of the attack was an anniversary of the birth or death of someone buried here, it would be inscribed on the tombstone, and we might find some connection to the person who was here on the day Fanny was killed.'

'It is a desperate grasp at a theory, Miss Bennet, and one that should require a great deal of tedium to test. Have you the patience to follow through on it, I wonder, or do you tell us this in the hopes that we shall inspect every grave to flatter your attempts at detective reasoning?'

'My powers of observation are great enough to apprehend how futile it would be to seek flattery from you, Mr Darcy,' replied Elizabeth. 'I have no intention of imposing the labour of my theory on anyone but myself, and certainly did not inform you of it to beg for assistance. I had commenced my investigation before you arrived, and have no wish to detain you from yours with my *desperate grasp at a theory*.'

'Well, if you should require any assistance, Miss Bennet, allow me to offer my services,' said Mr Bingley. 'I should be only too happy to help.'

'I thank you, no. I believe I shall get on well enough on my own. Please, Mr Darcy, do not delay your own examinations of the scene of account of my work. It is that headstone there, the plaque of Mr Robert Stapleton, on which Fanny is said to have struck her head.' Elizabeth pointed to a plot some twenty feet away. 'It is but four away from the graves of her parents.'

'I am aware of its location.' Mr Darcy bowed curtly. Before he walked away he gave her the most curious expression, the meaning of which Elizabeth could not determine at all; but she felt it most likely was intended to convey disdain, as that seemed to be the general purpose of his countenance.

With an apologetic smile and bow, Mr Bingley followed his friend. Elizabeth resumed her perusal of the tombstone dates, but found it difficult not to succumb to the distractions of the display put on by the two men. Mr Darcy, though austere in his general demeanour, sprung upon the grave site as though possessed of animal spirit and vigour. She could not resist, as she moved between headstones, looking up to behold him kneeling by Mr Robert Stapleton's grave and gazing at its edges with focused intent through a magnifying glass. He examined the ground with equal rigour and, to her amused astonishment, persuaded Mr Bingley to fall upon the ground from a variety of angles and positions.

The sun had begun its languid descent before Elizabeth and the gentlemen completed their separate investigations of the churchyard.

'I do hope you will allow Mr Bingley to stand at some point, Mr Darcy.' Elizabeth walked over to join the gentlemen and smiled archly as the detective measured the distance between his prone friend's head and the headstone. 'I have been half expecting you to have him don a lady's dress so that you might behold the manner in which his petticoat falls.'

'That indignity, I am happy to say, I have been spared. Thus far, at least.' Mr Bingley laughed. 'I hope your inquiries have been productive,' he said once he was given leave to resume his full altitude.

'Then I am very sorry to disappoint your hopes. I have found only three graves on which there is any correlation of dates, and I fear their occupants are too long deceased for any of the villagers to owe them any particular remembrance…'

'That was always to be expected,' said Mr Darcy. Elizabeth would have found his remark less galling if he had ungraciously gloated over her failure, but his matter-of-fact tone seemed somehow more disdainful.

'I should rather risk hours of fruitless inquiry than overlook any possible clue because I thought it unlikely or beneath my examination,' said Elizabeth. 'I cannot believe that there has never been a case solved through mundane and unimpressive facts. Not every crime is committed by ingenious means, nor can they all require great genius to comprehend.'

'Indeed, the majority of murders are committed for obvious motives by the simplest methods. However, I do not concern myself with such cases; or if I am called to assist in such an investigation, it is concluded with utmost haste,' said Mr Darcy. 'That I have come and have remained in the area more than a day should be proof enough for even you, Miss Bennet, that this is no ordinary case. Its solution will almost certainly be beyond anything an untrained mind can comprehend, no matter how earnest their endeavours.'

'Would you allow us to walk you home, Miss Bennet?' Mr Bingley offered. 'That is, of course, if your purpose here is quite complete.'

'I thank you for the offer, but I would prefer to walk alone. It is not far to Longbourn and I should not wish to impose any longer upon the time of such a great detective as Mr Darcy. I expect he shall have the whole mystery solved before dinner if not further delayed.'

'Satirical speech comes easily to you, Miss Bennet. You take delight when your meaning is in distinct opposition to your words.'

'It is fortunate then, Mr Darcy, that you can deduce everyone's meaning without any consideration of what they say.'

Mr Bingley coughed. 'I should much rather escort you back to Longbourn, Miss Bennet. I am sure I could not rest easy without knowing that you had safely returned to your family. What would your father think of me if he discovered we had met here and I had not walked you home?'

Elizabeth averted her eyes. She should infinitely prefer that her parents did not discover that she had been leaving the house in secret to pursue her investigations at all, let alone that she had required an escort to return her.

Mr Darcy observed the trace of guilt in her expression and understood her reluctance. 'We shall see you as far as the lane, Miss Bennet. Bingley can have no scruples that you should need an escort on your family's grounds, and allow me to reassure you that it shall be no impediment to the investigations which you have professed so strong a desire not to delay. I had every intention of walking over the churchyard environs and developing a familiarity with the surrounding roads.'

Together they left the churchyard. Mr Darcy's mind was occupied chiefly in observation, Elizabeth's much preoccupied with her thoughts, and it was left to the obliging Mr Bingley to carry the conversation for all three until they came into view of Longbourn.

5

Dinner at Barton Park was a grand affair, although there were no guests present other than Mr Darcy and Mr Bingley to enjoy Lady Middleton's extravagant hospitality. Owing to Sir John's prodigious appetite, and his wife's conviction that their station merited as much fashionable expense on the dinner table as in matters of dress and equipage, there was seldom a more lavish meal to be found in the county than those served at Barton Park, even when no guests were present at all.

Mr Darcy, however, paid no more attention to his ragout than had he to the white soup, and still less to the bountiful conversation provided by his hostess.

'How go your investigations, Mr Darcy? Have you made much progress, do you think?' Lady Middleton eventually struck upon a topic of interest to her guest, having failed to elicit any of his opinions as to the preference of town to the country, impressions of the neighbourhood and its denizens, or even the weather.

'To be sure, it's a complicated business,' declared Sir John. 'Foster and Granley have not made head or tail of it, and you know they are sharp enough fellows. Granley can sniff out a poacher faster than my best pointer!'

Mr Darcy refrained from sharing his opinion on the two constables Sir John had appointed in his role as magistrate. Sir John should have done better to leave Granley and Foster in their previous occupations as gamekeeper and under-gardener at Barton Park than expect the men to catch a murderer.

'My enquiries have not yet led to any substantial findings,' said Mr Darcy. 'Indeed, Bingley has found more use for his professional expertise than I on this day.'

'Indeed?' Lady Middleton turned her attention to the fair physician.

'Mr Darcy flatters my endeavours, but I hope that I have found a way in which I might be of some little service to one of the residents in the neighbourhood. Miss Bennet, it seems, suffers from a chronic cough. I have promised to call again tomorrow and take her a draught of my own concoction in the hope that it may provide some relief.'

'That is very good of you, I am sure,' replied his hostess. 'Mr Bennet is one of the few gentlemen of good family in these parts. It is so unfortunate that the estate is not what it once was. Still, I am comforted that none of their daughters have fallen prey to this dreadful business. How glad I am that my Maria is happily settled in town.'

Lady Middleton could not long be in mind of her

daughter or London without relating the pleasing details of the fine match her eldest daughter had made in Mr Rushworth and the fine house of which Maria was now mistress, and insisting that Mr Darcy and Mr Bingley must call on them when they returned to town as she was certain Maria should be delighted to receive them.

It was only much later, after Lady Middleton had retired from the drawing room and Sir John had fallen asleep in his chair by the fire, that Mr Bingley was at leisure to talk with his friend in confidence. He approached Mr Darcy as he stood by the window, smoking his pipe and staring out at the night. 'I suppose I shall be calling on the Bennets alone tomorrow, as no doubt you will be off investigating some matter or other.'

'On this matter, my dear Bingley, you are incorrect, for I am most intent on accompanying you to Longbourn.'

'I confess I am quite surprised. Whatever for? I can scarcely believe it is for the pleasure of the Bennets' society alone.'

'No, it is a curious turn of phrase used by Miss Elizabeth Bennet today when she referred to the headstone "*on which Miss Fanny Price is said to have struck her head*". It has most strongly provoked my suspicions.'

'I cannot imagine why.'

'Because, Bingley, it was readily apparent today that the victim's head never touched the headstone.'

'You astonish me, Darcy. Might I inquire as to how you can discern such a thing? Was not blood seen on the headstone, and did not the inquest find the injuries to the skull consistent with a forceful impact?'

'It is the location of the blood, Bingley, which is of singular significance. It was found on the top of the headstone and indeed I could detect traces of the stain there still. But if the victim had fallen forward, as suggested by the position in which she was found, her head would have struck the front of the headstone. Consider the height of the victim, and also the location of the injury on the side of the skull. If this was not proof enough, there is the final corroboration of the position of her arms at her side, not reaching out as is our instinctive compulsion to do upon falling.'

Bingley nodded. His admiration for his friend had not diminished throughout the many occasions on which he had witnessed such feats of perspicacity. 'I see you are right, Darcy. The murderer clearly wished to make this crime be considered the result of an accidental fall.'

'And so it was considered, just as Miss Charlotte Lucas was believed to have drowned. It was only the murderer's more overt violence in the second and third attacks that prompted anyone to suspect the first death.'

'With the exception of Miss Eliza Bennet,' observed Bingley. 'She suspected foul play from the first.'

'Precisely. And most insistent in telling us she had informed Sir John that she was convinced Miss Lucas was murdered.' Mr Darcy lifted the pipe to his mouth and inhaled deeply.

'Shows an excellent forethought of mind and desire to see justice done which I find most pleasing,' remarked Bingley.

'Perhaps in isolation it might be so considered,' said Mr Darcy, his eyes aflame, 'but consider also what her words at the churchyard implied: not merely a conviction that Miss Price had been murdered in a manner deliberately staged to suggest accidental death, but knowledge of how the act itself was accomplished.'

'If she has deduced that much on her own, then her investigations have proved most efficacious.'

'Bingley, I shall never understand why you are in such a rush to presume only the best of motives behind the actions of everyone you meet.'

'I dare say you are right, Darcy, but I cannot imagine any other interpretation in this instance.'

'Can you not? Remember, my dear Bingley, for every crime there is always at least one person who has complete and thorough knowledge of how the act was committed.' He looked at his friend with dark significance.

Bingley gasped. 'You cannot mean to say you suspect Miss Elizabeth Bennet of murdering three victims! I cannot believe it. They were her friends, were they not? Miss Charlotte Lucas, I believe, was a most particular one.'

'And who was it that took such pains to convince you of their friendship?'

Bingley blinked as he considered this. 'Well, I do believe it was the lady in question who mentioned it – but still, Darcy. Miss Elizabeth Bennet a murderess? How can you suspect such a thing?'

'At the moment, I suspect nothing. I simply observe, and my observations have raised questions. Firstly, how did Miss Eliza Bennet come to have such detailed knowledge of the death of Miss Price? Secondly, why, if she is innocent as you so gallantly insist upon believing, was she carrying a heavy candlestick concealed in her reticule?'

'Concealed candlestick? Darcy, you astonish me.'

'Was it not obvious from the manner in which she carried her reticule that it held a most substantial weight? The shape of the object contained therein was obvious at a glance. A most elementary observation.'

Mr Bingley shook his head. He knew his friend was always correct on these matters, but it pained him to suspect any lady, most especially the sister of Miss Jane Bennet. 'I can only hope that our visit will provide us with an innocent explanation that will acquit Miss Elizabeth Bennet of all suspicion.'

6

Mrs Bennet's thoughts that evening were similarly fixed upon the gentlemen's imminent return to Longbourn. It was apparent that Jane was quite taken with the charming Mr Bingley, and there could be no doubt that he admired her.

Elizabeth gave her mother less certainty. She had barely spoken two words together over dinner, and while Mrs Bennet did not grieve being deprived of her daughter's pert remarks, such behaviour signified a petulant nature that no gentleman could find agreeable. But then, Mrs Bennet consoled herself, Elizabeth was of such a peculiar disposition that perhaps the first signs of regard would manifest in her as sulks and ill-temper. Certainly Elizabeth had claimed more than her share of the conversation with Mr Darcy, and no young lady had any business speaking half so much to a rich, handsome gentleman if she did not mean to fall in love with him.

Mrs Bennet was thrown into a most alarming state

when she beheld her two eldest daughters in the breakfast parlour the next day, looking as though they had not slept an hour between them. What little poetry she had encountered had convinced Mrs Bennet that young girls should blossom under the influence of tender and romantic feelings. Surely the first inklings of love should at the very least produce a becoming glow in the cheeks and a sparkle in the eyes? And yet her elder daughters appeared before her with dark shadows about their eyes, and pallid complexions.

Mrs Bennet was therefore obliged to undertake great pains all morning to make the best of them that she could. She spared no thought at all to her own comfort as she laboured to improve their appearances. Indeed her fingers were quite sore after pinching their cheeks to induce some semblance of colour and glow. While Jane withstood all with great forbearance, Elizabeth complained as the pomade was brushed through her hair and flatly refused the bracing ablution of ice-chilled water, observing that while it may be beneficial for the complexion, it would not be so efficacious on her temper.

Eventually the hour when the gentlemen were to visit drew near. Mrs Bennet wished that she had longer to prepare them and could have afforded finer dresses, so that perhaps her daughters' clothing might provide an agreeable distraction from their faces.

'Mr Bingley ... and Mr Darcy,' she cooed as the gentlemen entered the dining room, the sincere pleasure in her voice dipping slightly as she greeted the latter. 'We are greatly honoured and delighted to see you again so soon.'

Lydia echoed her mistress's sentiments with excited yapping and an enthusiastic renewal of her acquaintance with the assortment of aromas upon Mr Bingley's fine boots. Mrs Bennet gestured for them to take seats near her eldest girls and Bingley readily obliged, though his friend preferred to move towards the window and stare out into the garden.

'I brought the elixir for Miss Bennet, just as you see,' Mr Bingley said, producing a brown glass bottle and giving it to Jane along with a sheet of paper. 'I have also written down the instructions for its dosage and administration, though I fear they may not be entirely clear – I expect I shall have to convey all explanations to you directly, in any case.'

'No, sir, you are too unkind on yourself, I am sure,' Mrs Bennet declared and snatched the paper from Jane to examine it for herself. 'Yes, I see now with my own eyes that you are too modest. I should say you have a very fine hand indeed. Such elegant and clear writing is seldom seen, I am certain of it. Do you not agree, Jane? Is it not the finest hand you ever saw?'

Jane blushed slightly as her mother pushed the paper back into her hands. 'It is indeed a most readily discernible hand and your instructions are entirely clear.'

Bingley laughed. 'Then I must allow your generous assurances to overpower my reservations. I am readily persuaded by your kind remarks that my writing might be considered as good as any other gentleman's. Would it were that all our deficiencies could be so easily dismissed by the flattering opinions of ladies!'

'Oh no, sir, it would be a disservice to my daughter to believe her capable of flattery, I assure you. Jane always speaks with absolute and unprejudiced honesty. Even when her feelings might urge her to favour a certain gentleman, as they do now, I am sure you would never find a fairer judge than my dear Jane.'

Jane cringed, but fortunately a gruff snort from Mr Darcy on the other side of the room was loud enough to distract attention away from this last remark.

'You forget, Mamma, Mr Darcy's opinions on the reliability of any lady's observations,' said Elizabeth. 'A lady's remarks on handwriting, as with horse colours, must necessarily be either mistaken or insincere.'

'I should not be so unjust as to consider Miss Bennet insincere,' said he. 'I believe she spoke the truth of her opinion; however, she looked with an eye more disposed to see merits than imperfections.'

'Oh, I am sure there is some truth in that, to be sure,' Mrs Bennet exclaimed. 'Jane is such a sweet girl. She cannot but see the good in everyone she meets, though I do not mean to say that her good opinion is too easily given. Indeed I have never known her to bestow a strong and instant partiality for any gentlemen before yesterday.'

Jane's mortification was apparent. Eager to spare her sister any further embarrassment, Elizabeth addressed Mr Darcy: 'Is it a general rule that all ladies perceive only the better qualities of what is before them? To what degree should they lower their estimations to correct for this natural defect?'

'There are certain ladies who should not fear their

opinions too generous,' replied Mr Darcy.

'Then I presume they must possess some other failing of perception or apprehension, for I dare not hope that any lady could be regarded as a reliable witness.'

'With some ladies it is not the validity of their information that is uncertain, but rather the circumstances of its attainment.'

'It is a fine morning, is it not?' Mrs Bennet interrupted. Though Elizabeth and Mr Darcy had spoken and looked at each other a good deal, there was nothing amiable in their manner. A change of scene was required if these two were to woo rather than quarrel. Elizabeth's temper always improved when she was outdoors and she was more likely to attract Mr Darcy if he was obliged to walk beside her rather than look directly into her face. 'The garden provides such agreeable walks. It seems a pity for them not to be enjoyed, does it not?'

'Indeed. I believe I am even more desirous of a walk on this day than the last.' Mr Bingley stood up and offered his arm to Jane. 'If you would be so kind as to accompany me?'

Jane nodded and happily took his arm.

Mrs Bennet looked pointedly at Mr Darcy. 'And are you fond of walks, too? I wager you would not often find a prettier gardens or more attentive company. Lizzy scarcely spoke at dinner, and now you are come she is all opinion and animation.'

Elizabeth winced. 'Mamma!' she hissed under her breath.

'I have no objection to a walk if Miss Bennet will oblige me.'

Elizabeth rose to her feet and quit the room with Mr Darcy, eager to escape further embarrassment.

They were a little distance behind Jane and Mr Bingley when a flash of beige fur darted between them.

'Lydia! Lydia! Come back at once!' Mrs Bennet's shrill voice carried well over the shrubbery, but the pug did not attend to it, preferring to dash about Mr Bingley's legs one moment and charge at the lavender the next. It was only when Lydia beheld her mistress calling with the added enticement of a tea cake that she returned to the house and the two couples were left alone in the garden.

Jane and Bingley fell into easy and mutually agreeable conversation and as she watched them walk from the window, Mrs Bennet thought they looked very well indeed and their smiles and looks conveyed all that she would wish for in young love. Elizabeth and Mr Darcy, however, displayed no such signs – at first. She thought she could just determine a hint of a smile playing upon Elizabeth's lips as they reached the edge of the avenue. Perhaps there was hope after all?

Mrs Bennet scooped up Lydia and kissed the top of her silken head. 'There now, Lydia, is it not all exactly as I planned?' she chuckled as she watched Mr Darcy and Elizabeth head down the gravel path beneath the overarching trees.

Elizabeth was determined that any conversation with Mr Darcy must stay focused on the specifics of the investigation. His general opinions, especially on the subject of her sex, were amusingly insulting, but she had no desire for diversion whilst a murderer still walked free.

'I have resolved to give you a full and frank account of all that I know relating to these atrocious crimes. I know full well you will find a dozen reasons to discredit any intelligence I relate, but I cannot rest easy until I have shared all I know that may be of some help in your investigation.'

'It is a noble sentiment, I am sure.'

'Yes, I flatter myself it is.' Elizabeth smiled. 'But I must own that I possess another more selfish motive, as well. I told you yesterday, did I not, that I had been conducting something in the way of amateur investigations myself. I believe it would be most instructive if I were to witness first-hand the questioning technique of such a renowned detective.'

'You did not find the questions put to you at the inquest sufficient for your edification?'

'Sir John is a most punctilious magistrate in matters that fall within the sphere of his understanding, but I expect most poachers do not require rigorous examination to convict, nor that any gentlemanly scruples would prevent him from questioning them thoroughly,' answered Elizabeth. 'Indeed, no pheasant need fear that their unlawful death should go unpunished – a paltry consolation, I suppose, but one of which the young ladies of Hertfordshire cannot yet boast.'

Mr Darcy smiled, but he soon overcame it. 'I can assure you Sir John is most determined to see justice done for these murders. He has brought me here at no little expense to ensure a swift conclusion. I cannot see what more you expect from a country magistrate.'

'I do not expect that he should undertake more expense upon himself, but I would have him less concerned for the fragile sensibilities of ladies and more for the pursuit of truth. It is a ridiculous form of gallantry that would seek to protect ladies' delicacies when lives are at risk.' Elizabeth snapped off a broken twig from an overhanging branch and waved it in her fingers.

'If you desire a frank and rigorous interview, I believe I can oblige. Indeed I came here with the purpose of extracting a full account from you.'

Elizabeth blinked and turned to regard his face. It was as stern as ever. 'Yesterday you said a lady's account was worthless, and now you wish to hear it? I cannot imagine what has affected such a transformation in your opinion.'

'You misreport my words and my meaning, for what purpose I cannot yet deduce. Perhaps it would be best if you were to begin by telling me in as plain and unembellished a manner as possible what happened on the day you discovered Miss Lucas.'

Elizabeth raised an eyebrow, but rather than take issue with the implication that she would embellish her report, she told him plainly of how she had first caught a glimpse of blue fabric in the water as they approached the lake; the angle and position of the body; how she had dragged Charlotte, cold and lifeless, to the bank; and how she had then sketched the scene while she waited for help to arrive.

Mr Darcy took pains to show no surprise or reaction to this last revelation. 'How long were you waiting?'

'At least ten minutes, I should think. It was quite long enough for me to complete a sketch of the scene.'

Mr Darcy looked over at her, but took care to conceal his scrutiny. 'For what purpose did you take it upon yourself to draw this unfortunate tableau?'

'I noticed a rather tangled arrangement of footprints in the dirt of the bank, and wished to take a record of them in case it rained or they became otherwise obscured. Indeed it looked as though some animals had already run over them. I thought the prints might be of material use in apprehending whoever was responsible.'

'You did not think it likely that she might have fallen into the lake by accident, or of her own volition?'

'No, that was impossible. Charlotte abhorred water. She would have never ventured close enough to fall in on her own account, and she was a most happy and sensible person. That she would take her own life is unthinkable.'

'I have heard many friends and acquaintances say that of unfortunate souls who did nonetheless commit the act of self-murder.'

'But it was more than my knowledge of my friend that convinced me of it being no accident,' insisted Elizabeth. 'Firstly, she was lying face up in the water, which seemed an unlikely position if she had fallen. Secondly, there was a tear in her left sleeve suggestive of a struggle – Charlotte certainly would have not left the house in such a state of dress. Thirdly, there was an abundance of water on the bank near the footprints, but little water on any other part of the bank that would indicate a fall into the water. Fourthly, the expression on her face was one of horror and disbelief. There was no resolution in it. For anyone to be so fixed to end their life that they would enter the water that frightened them and from will alone hold themselves below the surface until they drowned – such a level of unnatural determination would, I think, be evident in their face even after death.'

Mr Darcy raised an eyebrow. 'These points certainly are suggestive, although your last observation is mere conjecture based on your subjective interpretation of her expression. As a means of death, drowning often distorts the features. You cannot have had much previous opportunity to behold the faces of those who met this unfortunate end. You may have imagined more fear in her face than was there.'

'It is fortunate, then, that I did draw the scene. I hope you will credit my sketch with some objectivity, for I took pains to draw it most accurately. The footprints at least you cannot suppose have suffered from my subjectivity, as there is little emotion or character to perceive in the outline of a boot.'

'In that you are entirely wrong, Miss Bennet,' Mr Darcy declared. 'One clear set of boot prints might tell you everything you need know about a scene: the height and build of a gentlemen, his fortune and rank, the fastidiousness of his dress, his habits, his bearing and manner of walking, and most definitely, a sense of his character.'

'You make me feel quite the amateur, Mr Darcy. I shall endeavour to correct this failing with a rigorous study of all boots, calceology, and tracking; but,' she muttered, 'I would feel less displeasure in my ignorance if you took less pleasure in it.'

'I take no pleasure in the ignorance of others, nor should you feel any reproach in my correction. By apprehending as much as you did when you discovered Miss Lucas, you have set yourself far above your peers. To observe anything of import in such circumstances is rare; to understand what is seen is rarer still,' said he. 'Indeed there are only two types of people that possess such composure and quickness of mind in the face of violent death: detectives and murderers.'

'I hope you consider me in the former category, rather than the latter.'

Mr Darcy did not reply.

'You cannot believe me to have murdered my best friend?' Elizabeth laughed. 'It is too absurd. It is unthinkable that I could have done such a thing.'

'I believe nothing at this stage, Miss Bennet, but a detective does not possess the luxury of finding any possibility unthinkable merely because it is objectionable.'

'Upon my word, has this has been an interrogation? Have I fallen under the suspicion of the great Mr Sherlock Darcy?' she asked playfully. She would not give him the satisfaction of frightened looks and earnest protestations of innocence, no matter how stern and intimidating he tried to appear.

'Does it seem so ridiculous to you? Do you expect me to discount the possibility of your guilt simply because you possess some claims of friendship with the victims?'

'No, indeed. I see I make a fine suspect indeed. Not only did I find the first victim, but I callously took up my pencils and made a souvenir of the evil act. Then, no doubt unsatisfied by the opinion of the general populace that it was an accidental death, I must have struck again and again. With your own eyes you saw me attend the scene of the second crime. Do you suppose that I came to gloat over my past wrongdoings, or was my chief design to spy upon your investigations?'

'You take pleasure in making light of the situation, Miss Bennet?'

'I take pleasure in anything absurd. It is my nature to find amusement in ridiculing all that I know to be wrong,' said Elizabeth. 'But I take the crimes and this investigation most seriously. Indeed, I find I have increased incentive to find the culprit now. I must seek not only justice for my friends but also proof of my innocence.'

'I beg you would not take this duty upon yourself. I shall find the truth of these murders soon enough, and should do so more easily without your interference.'

'I have no intention of interfering with your investigation, Mr Darcy. I shall merely continue conducting my own. It would be foolish for me to suspend my efforts now that I understand them to be in my own interests.'

'You can have no hope of uncovering any evidence that should not be found the sooner by me, and indeed if you were to discover some pertinent fact, I could not rely upon its authenticity.'

Elizabeth's eyes narrowed as they approached the end of the avenue leading out into the garden. 'I will not be persuaded to do nothing by your erroneous suspicions.

My conscience forbids me to remain idle when I know full well that I am innocent and might be of some use. The odds of my finding the murderer before you might be very small indeed, even if you possess only half the investigative genius of your reputation, but I would risk even the slightest chance to find justice for Charlotte and the others.'

Mr Darcy, disgruntled at the implication that his skills might not equal his reputation, spoke in a tone that was brusque even by his standards. 'Such a wilful refusal to follow my advice on this matter implicates you, Miss Bennet, of a most inexcusable error. Either you intend to impede my investigation by interference or you vastly overestimate your own abilities. There is no chance of you discovering anything, much less the murderer, before me. I wonder that you cannot perceive the absurdity of your own conceit at playing detective. Perhaps you do not so readily perceive folly in yourself as you do in others.'

Elizabeth looked up at his supercilious face as they stepped into the garden. She was distinctly reminded of some rather smug crows she had taken much pleasure in chasing off the strawberry patch with an old broom. The thought struck her that she should take even greater enjoyment in dispatching Mr Sherlock Darcy from the garden in the same fashion, but lamentably there were no brooms in sight. 'My perceptive abilities are enough for me to see the inequity in yours. You can easily believe that a lady might be guilty of self-deception or even murder, but will not allow the possibility that she might prove a capable detective. Perhaps if you did not hold such a high opinion of your own abilities you would not consider them so out of the reach of others!'

'Enough has been said on this matter. I shall stay no longer. I see that reason holds no sway with you,' said Mr Darcy disdainfully as he turned back towards Longbourn.

'On the contrary, Mr Darcy, I have a high regard for reason, but I heard little of it in your conversation.'

'Indeed. You heard little of what was said and attended to none of it.'

'I have no wish to delay your departure, but I fear I must offer you the use of my drawings and the notes I have made these last weeks. When I solve this mystery before you, I shall not want it said that I had an unfair advantage in concealing my prior investigations.' Elizabeth smiled. 'That should greatly lessen my victory, should it not?'

'Such an implausible victory, Miss Bennet, should be nothing less than miraculous. I thank you for your offer, but I have solved a good many cases without the use of ladies' sketches.' Mr Darcy bowed curtly and took his leave.

Mrs Bennet, who had shifted her gaze from the happy pair of Jane and Bingley to her other daughter and her companion, was most pleased. She had seldom seen Elizabeth with a sweeter expression on her face as when the couple parted. Mr Darcy's countenance was as stern as ever, but there was a hint of colour in his cheeks. Mrs Bennet thought their walk must have been more successful than she had expected.

Indeed the smile did not leave Mrs Bennet's face

all day, not even when Mr Bingley and Mr Darcy left Longbourn to call upon Mr Woodhouse. The pleasure to be found in the scheming and execution of matchmaking, it seemed, was quite equal to murder.

Well – *almost* equal.

7

When Mr Darcy and Mr Bingley arrived at Hartfield, the Woodhouse residence, that afternoon, the household was in a state of elevated excitement and anxiety. Mr Woodhouse was so often beset with ailments that his servants and acquaintances had seldom an hour in his company in which they were not obliged to either hear of or attend to his health concerns.

Emma Woodhouse, his beautiful daughter, had died after a fall from her horse some three weeks earlier; in light of the other deaths, a most suspicious accident. Mr Woodhouse had confined himself to his room since the funeral and it was from his bed chamber that he delivered his requirements for palliative foods and tonics. Nevertheless, he was a welcoming host and no infirmity was enough to prevent him from making the acquaintance of Mr Darcy and Mr Bingley, or any other guest that might call at Hartfield.

Mr Woodhouse thought he might be very well set

up in the drawing room by the fire, and although the maid had fetched the wrong blanket for his legs, made his tonic too weak for his nerves, and his cook Serle had boiled his eggs too long for them to be considered safe for digestion, he was in a tolerable state to greet the gentlemen. He was well pleased with them for in their dress, deportment, and manner of introducing themselves they were very genteel, and Mr Bingley was exceedingly kind and courteous in the expression of his condolences.

'It is very good of you to call on me, Mr Darcy, Mr Bingley, and offer such thoughtful sentiments about my poor dear Emma,' said Mr Woodhouse. 'I am very happy to make your acquaintance. I understand from Sir James that you are a very important man, Mr Darcy, and have come all this way to assist him with this unfortunate business. Pray let Harriet help you both to a little bit of apple tart. You need not be afraid of unwholesome preserves here, although I do not recommend the custard at this hour.'

The young girl, a Miss Harriet Smith, rose from her seat and went to the table to oblige Mr Woodhouse's hospitality. Her intimacy with the Woodhouse family had begun a little over a year ago, some months after her fifteenth birthday. It had, Mr Woodhouse considered, been a most generous act on Emma's part to take such an interest in Miss Smith, a parlour-boarder at Mrs Goddard's school. Harriet was a sweet and obliging girl with red hair and a slight figure, and although she was very much inferior to Emma in beauty, charm and accomplishments, Mr Woodhouse had found her a most sympathetic and obliging companion. She had comforted him a deal during his mourning and indeed a day had not passed since Emma's death that she had not called at Hartfield. Nonetheless it surprised him greatly that Mr Darcy should show more interest in Harriet than the apple tart, which he dismissed with a wave of his hand.

'Miss Smith, I understand from Sir John that you suffered the misfortune of discovering Miss Woodhouse, did you not?' he asked.

'Yes, sir.' Harriet nodded, not daring to look at him.

Mr Woodhouse cried out, 'You must not distress Miss Smith! She was most devoted to my dear Emma.' He beckoned Harriet to his side and squeezed her hand reassuringly. 'You had best not talk to her of such things, Mr Darcy. She has suffered a good deal and you cannot think it wholesome for a young lady to dwell on such matters.'

'Perhaps, but I must insist that you permit me to speak with Miss Smith. If your daughter was the victim of some misdeed, surely you would wish me to ascertain all the facts that might allow me to find the person responsible.'

'Misdeed? Whatever can you mean? You cannot mean murder?' Mr Woodhouse blinked in confusion. 'Oh, no. Mr Darcy, that cannot be. Everyone loved Emma. You cannot think that anyone would wish to harm her…' He broke off with a trembling lip. 'Harriet, my dear, fetch me some of Perry's tonic.'

Harriet obliged and after a few tremulous sips Mr Woodhouse felt he was once more able to address the gentlemen.

'I am sorry, Mr Darcy,' said Mr Woodhouse. 'Your words have come as a shock. I am not in the best of health, you see, and I have suffered a great many tremors of the heart and other ailments since losing my Emma. If it were not for the tonics of Mr Perry and the comfort of such kind friends, I do not think I should have seen out these last few weeks. But if what you say is true – that it was no accident that took my dearest Emma, but a deliberate attack? Such wickedness, I cannot conceive of such wickedness!' He blinked, and a couple of tears leaked down his cheek.

'Be assured, sir, that Darcy will find whoever did this. You could not wish for a better detective than he,' said Bingley. 'And perhaps I might be of some assistance to you, Mr Woodhouse. If you will permit me, I believe I might help alleviate some of the tremors and palpitations you mentioned.'

Mr Woodhouse sniffed and regarded the doctor. 'That is very good of you, sir, but I suffer such a range of maladies and agitations to my nerves that I know not how you might remedy them all.'

'I shall be honoured if you will allow me to try.' He bowed.

Mr Woodhouse was most satisfied with this answer and nodded. 'Harriet, help me out of this chair – if you assist me, I think I might make it to the window. The light shall help Mr Bingley perceive the twitch in my left eye, for I am certain that is the cause of the headaches I suffer.'

'Allow Mr Bingley to help you, sir,' insisted Mr

Darcy. 'Harriet will stay here and talk with me.'

In age Harriet Smith was now sixteen years but in appearance she might have been a child, for she was small in stature and had a waif-like frailty and shyness about her. A less scrupulous detective might have felt uneasy about questioning so timorous a young lady on such distressing matters, but Mr Darcy was more than willing to oblige a frightened girl to speak in pursuit of the facts.

'Miss Smith, please relate the full particulars of the day on which you discovered Miss Woodhouse.'

'Emma went out riding every morning, sir. I went out to meet her. I thought perhaps I could wait for her at the edge of the woods and walk back with her, but alas I found her lying there, by a log.'

'And the horse?'

'The poor animal had taken fright and bolted through the woods,' said Harriet. 'It turned up at the stables in a terrible state. That's what alerted everyone here at Hartfield. Sanders, the stable-hand, informed Mr Woodhouse, and he send off a search party immediately. They discovered me in a state of great distress running through the woods and I took them back to where I had found her…'

Mr Darcy nodded. 'Indeed. Sir John has obliged me with a transcript of both your own and Sanders' accounts of the scene. I presume, Miss Harriet, that it was not your usual custom to walk out to meet Miss Woodhouse?'

Harriet shook her head. 'No, sir.'

'Then pray, what was your purpose in walking out to

meet her that day?'

Harriet looked around and saw that Mr Woodhouse and Mr Bingley were well away before she answered. 'I saw that a letter had come for Miss Woodhouse that morning when I arrived at Hartfield. I thought it would be no imposition for her to dismount and walk, so that she might read the letter as soon as may be.'

'Was Miss Woodhouse an impatient correspondent?'

'Impatient? No, sir.' Harriet shook her head. 'She was ever so good and kind. She was, I think, most particularly patient with me. She was fond of letters, though, and always wrote back as soon as may be.'

'And you took it upon yourself to venture into the woods on foot so that Miss Woodhouse might obtain her correspondence a mere half hour earlier?'

'Indeed. Miss Woodhouse was so good to me that I was eager to do anything that might assist her.'

Mr Darcy frowned. 'Had you any particular reason to suppose that Miss Woodhouse would desire to see this letter urgently? That she would rather interrupt her ride and read the letter outdoors than in the comfort of her home?'

Harriet flinched. 'Oh, I see. You believe that it would have been better for Miss Woodhouse if I had left the letter and not set out to meet her at all. That the last act I intended to do for my friend would have been a disservice to her.' Tears formed in Harriet's wide eyes and she bit her lip.

'Calm yourself, Miss Smith. I meant no slight on your intentions towards your friend. I simply wish to know if there was any reason you believed that Miss

Woodhouse should want to receive that letter promptly. Indeed, if there is anything you have not yet said about that day, you must unburden yourself of it at once. The slightest detail could be of the greatest import in this case – and I should find the person responsible for Miss Woodhouse's death all the sooner if you were open and frank.'

'Oh, but Mr Darcy, you cannot think that I would wish to hide anything that would be of service to you. I am sure I know of no person that would harm Miss Woodhouse, indeed I cannot think how anyone could not love Miss Woodhouse, so kind and generous as she was. No, it is too dreadful to imagine such a thing!' Harriet broke off in a fit of sobbing.

'Why, Miss Smith is crying,' observed Mr Woodhouse. He had feared for some years now that his sight was fading, but Mr Perry gave him a tonic to strengthen his vision and he was most careful only to read in the library or small parlour, for they had the best light, and thus he was quite able to perceive Miss Smith's distress from across the room. 'Mr Darcy, you must not question Miss Smith if it upsets her. I would not see the poor girl crying. Let me persuade you to take some refreshment instead. You had much better have some apple tart than question poor Miss Smith.'

'I am sure Mr Darcy will do his utmost to spare Miss Smith any distress,' said Mr Bingley, 'only it is most essential that he be allowed to ascertain if Miss Smith knows anything that might pertain to his investigations. Sir James has requested that he discover the truth behind these tragic events, and the circumstances surrounding

Miss Woodhouse's fall must be considered.'

'I see, I see…' Mr Woodhouse nodded sadly.

'I, however, am exceedingly fond of apple tart,' added Mr Bingley.

Mr Woodhouse brightened slightly at this information. 'Then you must try some of ours, Mr Bingley. It is most wholesome. You must not suppose that it should be too rich.'

Thus was Mr Bingley helped to a modest slice of apple tart and a more generous serving of Mr Woodhouse's views on the beneficial fruit, leaving Mr Darcy free to continue questioning Miss Smith. She rallied somewhat and was able to withstand the most routine line of questioning: was anyone seen or noticed in the woods, was there anything unusual to be seen in the vicinity or in Miss Woodhouse's behaviour that morning? Her answers, as Mr Darcy had anticipated, informed him of nothing he had not already known, but Miss Smith's growing discomfort spoke volumes.

At length Mr Darcy felt he had had enough of fruitless inquiry, and asked if Mr Woodhouse would arrange for the stable-hand to accompany him and Bingley to the location where Miss Woodhouse had been found. He had no wish to impose upon the family any longer. Mr Woodhouse released the good physician from the duty of hearing his various complaints, but only on the understanding that he was to call again the next day with some efficacious draughts for his nerves, as he was quite convinced that Mr Bingley understood nerves every bit as well as his apothecary, Mr Perry, and Mr Bingley should of course stay to dinner, and he hoped

Mr Darcy would, too.

Their investigations at the site where Miss Woodhouse had met her unfortunate end were extensive, but the path had been travelled a good deal in the intervening weeks and Mr Darcy detected little in the way of physical evidence. Sanders was an obliging fellow but his recollections lacked detail and Mr Darcy soon sent him back to Hartfield. After some twenty minutes of inspecting the log by which Miss Woodhouse had been found, Mr Darcy declared to Bingley that they should endeavour to recreate Miss Woodhouse's fatal ride through the woods.

'I say, Darcy, you have been uncommonly quiet,' remarked Bingley after Darcy had brought his fifth ride through the woods to an abrupt conclusion by springing out from behind a chestnut tree to startle the horse.

'She knows something, Bingley,' said Darcy. 'I am convinced of it.'

'Who?' Bingley asked. Riding through the woods so that Darcy might hide and jump out at him from a variety of concealed locations had left Bingley in no state to surmise the subject of his friend's remark.

'Miss Smith. She was holding something back. I am sure of it! Some little secret she does not wish Mr Woodhouse to know.'

'Surely not. Would not any lady devoted to a friend be only too eager to do whatever she could to assist the investigation?'

'I do not doubt that Miss Smith wishes to be of service to my inquiries, but there is another reason for her silence. Perhaps a confidence she shared with Miss

Woodhouse that she will not break after death.'

'Then we must assure her that Miss Woodhouse would be better served by her telling us what she knows. The burden of such a secret must be weighing on the poor girl's conscience.'

Darcy smiled at his friend. 'Bingley, you possess a remarkable ability to believe every necessary aspect of an investigation is in service to the individuals connected with the case, not merely the pursuit of the truth. However, I concur that Miss Smith should be easily persuaded that she must unburden her conscience for her cousin's sake, as well as her own, if we were to speak to her without Mr Woodhouse's attendance.'

'We must hope that such an opportunity presents itself during tomorrow's visit.'

'Indeed, and if an opportunity does not appear, we shall avail ourselves of one of our own design. I believe our investigations of the *locus delicti* have reached their conclusion for now.'

'I am relieved to hear you say that, Darcy.'

Darcy looked his friend up and down. Mr Bingley looked a little worse for wear, though he had only fallen from his horse twice in their investigative endeavours. Darcy rubbed his hands and then set to mounting his own horse. 'We had best make haste to Barton Park if you are to have time to make yourself presentable for dinner.'

Bingley leaned forward and gave his horse an affectionate pat on the neck. 'What do you think, old boy? The promise of extra oats for you and a fine dinner for me should see us back in no time.'

Darcy and Bingley spurred their horses and with great haste returned to Barton Park.

Pertinent facts and incriminating information were seldom obscured for long in the face of Mr Darcy's legendary powers of observation. This was fortunate, as he had an impatient mind and restless disposition. He retired that night confident that a return to Hartfield would yield the clues he sought. Thus he was somewhat disconcerted the following morning when, without further questioning or observation or even a full breakfast, the footman brought him a letter from Miss Harriet Smith.

Dear Mr Sherlock Darcy,

I hope you will not think it so very terrible of me to write to you and relate some more of what I know concerning my dear friend Miss Woodhouse. I know it was wrong of me not to answer your questions with as full and complete knowledge as I was able to give, but I hope you will forgive me when I say that it was a sense of duty to a beloved friend that prompted me to hold my tongue. However, Mrs Goddard came upon me crying yesterday after our meeting at Hartfield and asked me whatever was the matter…

Mr Darcy grimaced as he skimmed over the next half a page of Harriet's lengthy account of her conversation with Mrs Goddard. He was much relieved to discover, eventually, that the woman had enough sense to advise Harriet to share what she knew.

…she says that you are the most celebrated detective in England, and that it is my duty to relate every

thing that I know to you. I cannot see how the very little I know will be of help, perhaps as great a mind as yours will perceive some information of use in my account.

The letter which arrived for Miss Woodhouse on that most terrible of days was indeed one I thought she would most particularly wish to read with utmost haste. I believed it to be from a certain gentleman, Mr Frank Churchill, a most handsome and charming gentleman who had formed a sincere attachment to Miss Woodhouse when he stayed with Mr Weston for some weeks last year. I was convinced it must contain a profession of his love and admiration for Miss Woodhouse, and it was this belief that persuaded me to walk out to find her, knowing that it would be easier for her to read such a letter away from Hartfield for Mr Woodhouse, you see, is quite against marriage. He was most upset when Miss Taylor, Miss Woodhouse's governess, was married to Mr Weston, and I do not know how he would have borne it if he believed Miss Woodhouse were to marry and to leave Hartfield.

Please do not think me wrong to have concealed such a letter. I wished only to spare Mr Woodhouse further suffering, and poor Mr Frank Churchill, too. He must have suffered so cruelly at the news of Emma's accident and I would not wish to cause him further pain by revealing his letter. I am sure he must have grieved as cruelly as any gentleman who ever felt the deepest and most ardent love. When I saw him at her funeral, he was very much changed in appearance. Indeed I would have hardly known him so altered was he from the grief and shock, and he stayed but two days with Mr Weston before he left to return to his Aunt.

Confounded girl, thought Mr Darcy. What foolishness, to concealed such information and then, once persuaded to reveal it, to bury the facts in swathes of sentimental nonsense. With an air of irritation, his eyes glanced over the next page until they came across further intelligence not wholly pleasing to him.

It was the day following the most terrible morning on which sweet Miss Woodhouse was taken from those who loved her dearly that the Bennets called to pay their respects. They were very kind, and Jane and Elizabeth paid particular attention to me. At length we were permitted to speak alone, and Elizabeth, who sensed that I was distressed under the weight of a secret, persuaded me to tell her what I knew. Knowing both her and Jane to be childhood friends of Miss Woodhouse, I felt it would not be wrong to confide in them and so I showed them the letter of whose existence no one but myself was as yet aware.

Miss Elizabeth B. was kind enough to relieve me of the letter and assured me that she would make discreet enquiries to ascertain whether Mr Churchill was still in town, and that if he was, she saw no need to publicly reveal a letter that could only give pain in such circumstances.

Miss Elizabeth Bennet! Interfering in his case before he had even stepped foot in Hertfordshire! It was too much to be borne.

'Pray, might one enquire as to the nature of your letter?' asked Lady Middleton, observing Mr Darcy glowering at his correspondence.

'Simply a matter relating to my inquiries,' replied Mr Darcy, recomposing himself to continue with this provoking missive.

Miss Elizabeth B. assured me that I had acted in service to my friend and my relief was so great that I cried and said that there was no duty I would not happily perform if it might be of some small assistance to Miss Woodhouse. Upon hearing this, she informed me of a scheme wherein I might be of assistance in ascertaining the manner of my friend's death. I was to gather Emma's clothes and go to the very place in the woods in which I discovered her. The maid, Mabel, would take Miss Woodhouse's place for she was of a similar height, and I would instruct her how she should arrange her limbs and her clothes to reconstruct the scene so that Miss Elizabeth B. could draw it! I know that this must seem a most shocking and improper scheme to you, Mr Darcy, but please consider how deeply we all cared for Miss Woodhouse. I am sure I should partake in any degradation or desperate measure if it might help my cousin. It was a most distressing thing to be obliged to recall a scene I should dearly wish to forget but I know not of any hardship that holds comparison to the loss of my dearest, sweetest Miss Woodhouse.

I hope you will not think too ill of me, sir, and will forgive any wrongs I have committed when I most sincerely say that all I did, I did for Miss

Woodhouse.
Miss Harriet Smith

'Mr Darcy, I cannot imagine what is in the letter of yours. You look most decidedly put out,' said Lady Middleton. 'I do hope it is not another invitation away from Barton Park. It must be so tedious for you to be so imposed upon and obliged to dine away from Barton Park so frequently. Sir John and I have scarcely enjoyed your company two nights together, and Mr Bingley has informed me you are to dine with Mr Woodhouse this evening.'

'Be assured there is no invitation contained herein.' Mr Darcy folded the letter and slipped it in his pocket. 'However, there are some other matters pertaining to the investigation that require my prompt attention. Pray excuse me.'

'Surely whatever it is can wait, Mr Darcy. You have scarcely eaten a morsel.'

'I thank you, no.' Mr Darcy stood, bowed, and left Lady Middleton feeling that housing a celebrated detective was turning out to be a very dull business indeed.

8

Mrs Bennet was quite out of temper.

As was her habit, she had visited Mr Woodhouse that morning. As a general rule she enjoyed calling upon Mr Woodhouse, for the gentleman was a generous man and so dull of wit that he could readily be persuaded to believe anything, except his own good health. However, upon hearing that Darcy and Bingley had stayed for some time at Hartfield the day before and had agreed to return this very evening for dinner, the searing resentment Mrs Bennet had felt when she killed Emma Woodhouse returned once more.

'Mr Woodhouse has quite persuaded Mr Bingley to attend to his every whim,' Mrs Bennet complained to her family as soon as she entered the drawing room. 'He is to see him every day and I am sure he shall never be cured so long as such attentions are bestowed upon him.'

Lydia, sensing her mistress' ill humour, ran to her

side. Mrs Bennet picked up her faithful pug, but she was a great deal too restless to sit, so Lydia found herself enduring a jostled ride about the room.

'It is very good of him to take so much care over the well-being of so many in the neighbourhood,' said Jane. 'Mr Woodhouse has never enjoyed a robust constitution and since the death of poor Emma he has suffered a great many complaints. I hope Mr Bingley is able to provide some relief.'

'Fie, girl! Have you no sense of your own interests?' Mrs Bennet shrieked. 'If Mr Bingley is to spend all his time with Mr Woodhouse, he shall see Harriet *every day*. Harriet will set her eyes on Mr Bingley. You ought to be sensible of the competition you face.'

Jane coloured. 'I have no claims on Mr Bingley. He has shown me kindness, and I believe I have felt better since I began taking his draughts; that is all.'

'You would do better not to tell him of such improvements, or he shall never come again!'

'You cannot expect Jane to wish herself ill in the hope that it will bring Mr Bingley here,' observed Elizabeth. 'Nor can you expect him only to care for patients without marriageable young ladies for companions.'

'I would wish him to have more sense than to fall for Mr Woodhouse's contrived ailments and the schemes of the Smith girl.' Mrs Bennet stopped in front of her two eldest daughters. 'However, all is not yet lost. I should prove a very poor mother indeed if I allowed a mere parlour-boarder to snatch a pair of potential husbands away from my girl. Do not worry, Jane and Lizzy, I shall make Mr Bingley and Mr Darcy return to Longbourn soon enough.'

'I cannot thank you for my share in such a favour. I should not care for another visit from Mr Darcy and there would certainly be no advantage in one,' said Elizabeth. 'His opinion of me falls with every encounter. To further the acquaintance would only see him condemn me as the most deplorable female that ever walked the Earth.'

Mr Bennet chuckled and looked up from his book. 'Well, now, Lizzy, if that is so, I should be very much pleased. While as your father, I would not wish any gentleman to ever malign you in thought or speech, I find it exceedingly gratifying that the eminent Mr Darcy should be wrong on occasion.'

'Oh, Mr Bennet, you are quite as bad as Lizzy! How much easier my life would be if the two of you could be prevailed upon to talk sense and not always make a joke of such serious matters,' exclaimed Mrs Bennet. 'Do you not see? It is essential that Mr Darcy should think well of Lizzy if she is to secure him.'

Elizabeth laughed. 'Secure him? I do not know whom such a scheme should grieve more: myself or Mr Darcy. If you are determined to see him marry, you shall need to find him another wife. I cannot imagine what sort of lady would make a fitting match for such a severe, disdainful character; she would certainly be a fearsome creature to behold.'

'You would ridicule my endeavours to see you comfortably settled and do nothing for your own good? Such ingratitude! Mr Darcy may well be a proud, disagreeable sort of man, but he has shown more interest in you than any other gentleman has before – or is likely to in the future.'

'That may be so, but I can you assure you that there is nothing of a romantic nature in his interests. He has come to Hertfordshire on account of the murders alone, and I expect that at the completion of the investigation he shall quit the village without any thought of marriage ever entering his head.'

'I shall not waste my kindness on such an ungrateful daughter,' declared Mrs Bennet, to the disbelief of the others. None of the family could believe that Elizabeth would remain free from her mother's matchmaking for long. 'Jane, we shall take the carriage into Meryton this morning. There is no purpose in staying home if Bingley will not come. We shall see what powders and concoctions Mr Perry has to enhance your appearance. Mary, Kitty, you may come too, for you have been good girls.' Mrs Bennet gave Elizabeth a most pointed look.

Thus the morning was arranged to the satisfaction of all the Bennets. Jane was happy to please her mother and distract her from unkind speculations about Mr Bingley. Mary and Kitty were eager to go to Meryton, where Mary might buy an improving book and Kitty an unflattering bonnet. Mrs Bennet was convinced the apothecary would have some titivating treatment for Jane. Lydia enjoyed the prospect of any outing where she might lean her head out the carriage and bark at passers-by. Mr Bennet would be left in peace in his library, and Elizabeth could pursue her investigations.

It was not long after Mrs Bennet set out that Mr Darcy left Barton Park with the intention of calling on

Longbourn. In truth it was not a visit which he anticipated with any pleasure. He had once been obliged to disguise himself as a beggar and live in squalor for three days to solve a case, and had on more than one occasion lain hidden in the most uncomfortable locations to observe and apprehend criminals. However, such inconveniences paled in comparison to the task that lay before him: either to demand the letter from Miss Elizabeth Bennet, or to request it. It was to be expected that either approach would be met with amusement or defiance; or more likely, and more perplexingly, both. He had no little curiosity about the drawing she had made following Miss Smith' descriptions, but how could he ask to see it without giving encouragement to her investigative aspirations? Worse yet, if Miss Elizabeth Bennet herself was the killer, how could the drawing be relied upon? Who knew what subtle falsehoods she might have inserted into the portrait to mislead him? Certainly, Miss Smith would not have had the wit to detect them.

His ride through Meryton was chiefly occupied with unwanted meditations upon the very great irritation that Miss Elizabeth Bennet provoked in his disciplined mind, when he observed the reticule and shoes of the lady in question beside a tree not far from the road.

He brought his horse to a halt and secured it to a tree on the far side of the road before walking closer, so that he might look down the sloped embankment leading to the river. There he espied Miss Bennet stomping around the bank in a pair of gentlemen's boots. He stood beside one of the large trees whose tall branches stretched over the river, watching the extraordinary scene.

Elizabeth held a drawing in her hands and glanced between it and the ground as she moved in awkward steps. The sight afforded him great pleasure; he considered it most agreeable to behold a woman who would dare to ridicule him looking ridiculous herself. It was some time before she sensed his presence and looked up with a start.

'Mr Darcy?' Her expressions moved through surprise and embarrassment before returning to her customary playful defiance. 'I hope you have not come to condemn me of any crimes at present for I am much occupied in my study of footprints, as you see.'

'Good day, Miss Bennet.' He raised his hat. 'I had wondered to what purpose you had engaged yourself in such undignified activity.'

Through no little strength of restraint, she ignored his supercilious tone and made an awkward curtsey in her ill-fitting boots. 'After I beheld you and Mr Bingley yesterday re-enacting the circumstances of Fanny's attack, I thought I might try a similar approach. My intention is to recreate the set of footsteps from the drawing I made.'

He nodded. 'A reasonable theory, although it was never my intention to inspire an insalubrious endeavour, Miss Bennet, and I fear you will find the task before you an onerous one. Footprints are not so easily deciphered as you might have anticipated.'

'Perhaps not. I should make better progress if the ground were not so hard, but it has not rained in days and the boots leave little impression on the dirt.'

'Your attempted study does not proceed well, then?'

'Not yet, but I should caution you from taking any premature pleasure in my failure. It is my intention to remain here until I fully apprehend the movements that took place on the day Charlotte was murdered.'

'I should never take pleasure in a failure to ascertain any facts pertinent to an investigation, not even when such inquiries are undertaken by the most inappropriate persons and cumbersome methods.' He made his way down the bank to her. 'Indeed, allow me to offer my assistance. If you are to insist on this endeavour, you should at least conduct it correctly. It pains me to see the scene of a crime examined so ill.'

She regarded him with evident suspicion. 'Why should you offer to help me? You suspect me of being guilty of these most abhorrent and brutal murders, do you not? I believe you told me I should desist in my investigations.'

'I gave you excellent advice that you have, unsurprisingly, not heeded. There is only one offence of which I know you to be guilty: the concealment of the letter that arrived for Miss Woodhouse and which Miss Smith entrusted to your keeping.'

'Then Harriet has spoken to you of it? I hope you did not frighten her in your questioning. She has suffered too much already.'

'And yet you had her return to the very spot she discovered her cousin, and instructed her to recreate the event which was the source of her suffering?'

'Yes, I did. Perhaps it was a little hard on Harriet, but she could not tell me anything of use. I thought that returning to the scene would prove beneficial to her memory, and it was. I suppose I am now to be much censured for this.'

'On the contrary, your resourcefulness and ingenuity do you credit. Concealing evidence that may prove essential to the case does not.'

'I offered freely yesterday to share everything I knew – an offer you rejected.'

'You did not divulge the existence of the letter, only drawings and notes of your own making.'

'Perhaps if you had not been so intent on accusing me, I might have had opportunity to furnish you with a full inventory of the evidence I have obtained,' Elizabeth remarked. 'However, I have no wish to keep anything from you and will happily give you the letter and anything else that might be of assistance in your investigations. Do you wish for me to oblige you with a detailed list of all correspondence in my possession, or is it only love-letters to deceased ladies which interest you?'

'The potential significance of the letter cannot be lost on you and it is disingenuous to pretend otherwise. It was wrong of you not to inform me of it and such concealment suggests you had your own motives for hindering my investigation.'

'Believe me, if there had been any possibility of it being of use, I should have placed it in your hands as soon as you stepped foot in Longbourn,' insisted Elizabeth. 'I wrote to my aunt, Mrs Gardiner, nearly three weeks ago, and her letter informed me that Mr Churchill was in London on the day of Emma's death. There was no possibility of him being anywhere near Hertfordshire and I had no wish to bring unnecessary discredit to his reputation or hers.'

'It would seem that this entire neighbourhood values discretion over justice.' He scowled. 'You will oblige me though, Miss Bennet, by giving me any and all correspondence, documents, drawings, and whatever other materials in your possession that may have any connection to this case.'

'Such direct and unequivocal orders, Mr Darcy,' she observed, showing more amusement at the severity of his tone than even she dared to feel. 'I suppose I am to be flattered into obedience by the prospect of you condescending to deem my investigations of being some use?'

'There is little compliment in it. I wish to ascertain how injurious your interference may have been to my case.'

Elizabeth laughed. 'You think I am more likely to be persuaded by such an insult to my efforts?'

'I do not attempt to persuade you of anything. If you truly wish for justice for the three murdered ladies and the future safety of the area, you will hand over the evidence.'

'That is most unfair. You would have me either follow your every instruction or be an enemy to justice, my unfortunate friends, and the neighbourhood entire? You must recognise that a temperament such as mine finds it prodigiously difficult to obey orders. Could you not feign some consideration of my pride and simply ask me for assistance?'

'I am not in the practice of begging for evidence from suspects, still less from young ladies who have taken it into their head to play detective!'

She glared at him. 'I expect you have by no means exhausted your supply of insults, Mr Darcy, but I am quite out of humour to hear them. I must bid you good day and return to the task at hand. I have much more to accomplish at *playing* detective.'

She turned back to her drawing, determined to ignore him. That she was truly offended would have been apparent to a gentleman far less perceptive than Mr Sherlock Darcy.

He cleared his throat. 'Perhaps, Miss Bennet, it might be best if we were to consider a mutually beneficial exchange. I shall assist you in your understanding of the configuration of footprints and then you will comply with my *request* to receive whatever materials you have in your possession that relate to my investigation?'

'It seems a satisfactory arrangement. We shall both do something we had already offered to do, without any pretence of compliment or civility in the matter.' She held out the drawing before her so that he might examine it over her shoulder.

'It seems a good likeness of the area. The proportions and incline of the embankment are well represented,' said Mr Darcy.

Elizabeth shifted with slight discomfort at his closeness, feeling as though he were regarding her with equal scrutiny as the drawing. 'I believe we should start at the rise of the bank. It is clear that is where the altercation began, with the attacker advancing forward as Charlotte moved back.' She took the sketch and marched to the top of the bank.

'I believe the reconstruction should be more successful if you put the drawing aside, Miss Bennet. It is apparent from the closeness of the footprints that they grappled and if you are to play the assailant, your arms must be free to grab your victim.'

'You wish me to take the part of the murderer?'

'You are wearing the boots of a gentleman that you selected for their similarity to the tracks in your sketch, did you not? In any case, I should be uncomfortable allowing you to scramble backwards down the bank. I have no desire to fish you out of the stream.'

She handed the sketch over to Mr Darcy. 'Very well. Perhaps you might hold the drawing, then.'

'We have no need of the drawing. You observed the scene well enough to draw it and have examined the sketch a good many times since, I expect. You must commit the tracks to memory and leave your eyes free to observe those aspects of the scene that appear through movement and cannot be captured in a still portrait.'

'Yes, I expect I know the tracks well enough, but do you, Mr Darcy? You cannot have looked at the drawing for more than a few seconds.'

'Thorough observation is dependent on the faculty of mind, Miss Bennet, not duration of time.'

Elizabeth put down the sketch and secured it under a rock. Mr Darcy assumed his position, standing where the first clear print of Charlotte's feet had been. Elizabeth drew in a deep breath and faced him.

It is not so very improper, she told herself; they would be obliged to stand with little more intimacy of position and contact than if they were dancing. And yet she could not feel composed about the prospect of charging Mr Darcy and seizing him about the arms.

'Come now, Miss Bennet, an investigation of this nature allows no time for hesitation,' said Mr Darcy, and if her determination to discover what had happened to Charlotte was not enough to overcome her reticence, the goading expression upon his face was more than sufficient.

Elizabeth launched herself towards him; her hands availed themselves of his upper arms and they moved down the bank with turbulent alacrity. It was no little credit to Mr Darcy's dexterity that he maintained a most correct, upright posture and grace of movement as they hurtled towards the river, taking precise small steps to mirror the victim of the original assault.

Their footwork grew in complexity as the ground levelled. They spun and veered to one side then the next as victim strove to break free of attacker. The footsteps demanded closer proximity now. With a final surge of violent force, Elizabeth drove him back towards the water. The murderer must have overpowered poor Charlotte here, and thrust her into the river. Elizabeth made the final push but owing the difference in their height and stature, she achieved nothing more than to walk into Mr Darcy as he came to an abrupt standstill. She looked up at him, breathless from the exercise, and their eyes locked in synchronous understanding of how the rest of the violent crime had played out.

Elizabeth released her grip and stepped back, embarrassed by the unintended intimacy of the collision;

but even that discomfort was soon displaced by her new understanding of her friend's murder.

'The murderer must have placed his hands about Charlotte's throat,' said she, once again returning his gaze. 'At the last moment, standing here, he moved his hands to her neck, or her head, as he forced her down into the water. How terrified she must have been. Poor Charlotte…'

Mr Darcy nodded. 'It is only speculation – but that would be the easiest way to force a controlled descent into the water. If the struggle had been prolonged, it would have resulted in a greater disturbance of the riverbank.'

'I might have gained a more complete understanding of how easily Charlotte was overcome here if we had reversed roles. I confess I am a little disappointed I could not manage to move you even a little way into the water.'

'It would have been of no benefit to the investigation, Miss Bennet. The particulars of the struggle depend upon the relative strengths and experience of victim and murderer. Without knowing the abilities of the attacker for certain, it is impossible for me to ascertain to what degree I should reduce my capabilities to replicate their actions. Speculation is no substitute for observation.'

'I suppose then, by your estimation, the exercise was of no advantage.' She turned and started walking back up the bank of the river.

Mr Darcy followed at her side and offered her his arm as they walked up the incline. 'On the contrary, I am obliged to you in one regard. Both your drawing and this re-enactment have brought one particular aspect to my attention.'

'I do hope it is some trifling detail. It would be a coup for such an overlooked and mundane fact to enjoy the notice of a celebrated detective.'

She turned to face the rebuke she expected for her teasing, but none came; and she could not make out any signs of disapproval in his circumspect countenance.

'It is the curious irregularity of the boot prints,' said he. 'Observe your drawing. The heel of each boot print is clearly discerned, but the impression of the front is incomplete on many of the steps; and yet the other prints, those of the victim, are represented in their entirety.'

Elizabeth picked up her drawing. 'I promise you that it is an accurate account of what I saw that day.'

'Indeed, I believe it is so. It is to your credit that you did not seek to rectify the poor prints in your drawing. For one so prone to speculation, and who so frequently finds amusement in professing opinions which are not your own, you are a faithful artist.'

Elizabeth laughed. 'Upon my word, Mr Darcy, can you not find it in yourself to say one nice thing about me without counterbalancing the compliment with twice its weight in censure?'

'Not when the criticism is in itself a compliment. If I believed your abilities were of a common quality, I should not often take the time to critique them. It is only those who possess the capacity for thorough observation and deduction who benefit from instruction and an awareness of their faults.'

'As disingenuous as you would believe me to be, I shall not pretend to be insensible of that compliment.' Elizabeth placed the drawing down with her reticule and began to remove her father's old riding boots. 'I suppose that you have inferred some significance about the killer from the boot prints. It cannot be a limp, as I discerned no difference between the right and left feet. Indeed—' she paused as she extracted the extra socks she had crammed down the large boots and looked down at the faint impressions she had left on the bank, 'I cannot even perceive a very great difference between the marks I made and the ones I saw that day.'

'Precisely, Miss Bennet.'

She looked up at him and smiled. 'Of course! The murderer was in disguise! He must have worn boots that were not his own.'

Elizabeth returned her feet to her own half-boots, and gathered her things. Darcy extended a hand and helped her to her feet. 'I should think the murderer was wearing boots at least two inches too long, and they most likely placed some material into the front of them to allow steady movement, as you did yourself.'

'What was the design in such a disguise?' asked Elizabeth as they made their way up towards the road. 'Did the killer seek to conceal his identity, lest he be observed from the road, or was it that he did not wish Charlotte to recognise him?'

'I would encourage you not to speculate on this at present, Miss Bennet. There are far more significant questions that have yet to oblige me with an answer.'

Elizabeth regarded his expression, which was one of

knitted brows and darkly contemplative eyes, but he ventured no further remark. 'I suppose you are referring to how Charlotte came to be beside the river?'

'No; it is obvious she was chased from the road by her attacker. The rip you observed in her dress was likely a consequence of its snagging upon a tree as she ran by.' He led her to the tree from beside which he had first beheld her, and pointed to a broken branch not much lower than her shoulder. There, buried in the creviced bark, was a blue thread.

'I should have thought to look for such a clue.' Elizabeth slid her hand down the tree and rapped it against the trunk in frustration. 'It might have persuaded Sir John that Charlotte's death was no accident far earlier. How many other details have I failed to see?'

'It is more important to me to ascertain what you have discovered than what you have not,' replied Mr Darcy as they walked towards the road.

'Oh yes, my notes and drawings. No doubt you are eager to have them in your possession so that you might observe their innumerate faults. Will you come now to Longbourn, or would you have me send them to Barton Park?'

'I would not wish to return thence without them in my possession.'

'It is good, then, that my mother and sisters are in Meryton. We shall find only my father at home and he shall not incommode our transaction.'

'Transaction, do you call it?' Mr Darcy looked at Elizabeth before untying his horse so that he might lead it as they walked the road together.

'Indeed, Mr Darcy. I expect to be repaid with a detailed account of the errors of my drawings and the defects of my investigation thus far. I quite depend upon your censure if I am to improve my methods of detection.'

They discussed the investigations with much enthusiasm on the walk back to Longbourn, although Mr Darcy took care to impress upon Elizabeth how little progress she had made and how unequal her abilities were to his, so much so that she should be better to quit her efforts entirely. Elizabeth was more than equal to meeting every censure with a laugh or pert response, and her determination to investigate only grew with his every attempt to dissuade her. However, for all her ambition as an aspiring detective, Elizabeth did not perceive the dark suspicion in Darcy's eyes or observe how frequently he looked at her. That she had perfectly matched every footstep in their recreation on the riverbank weighed greatly on his mind. Either she possessed a rare gift of mental control and flawless memory, or today was not the first occasion on which Miss Elizabeth Bennet had trod the footprints of a murderer.

His suspicions were growing stronger and yet they brought him none of the usual excitement of a mounting investigation; only regret, and the need to remind himself of the danger in esteeming her or finding pleasure in her company.

At length they arrived at the gates of Longbourn and took the gravel walk towards its sombre stone walls. Elizabeth believed she had learnt a good deal in her conversation with Mr Darcy. She felt that so long as she replied to his reproofs playfully, so that he could not believe she regarded them with any degree of seriousness, she might glean much knowledge and expertise from his criticism.

Mr Bennet had been greatly enjoying the peace afforded him by an afternoon alone in his library. Mr Darcy's arrival was a pleasure he had not expected and one he would have very happily forgone. He felt the burden of the intrusion most acutely when, not long after he had been obliged to leave the comforts of his library, his daughter Elizabeth announced that she must fetch some drawings for Mr Darcy and he was left alone with the man in the sitting room.

'Am I correct in assuming you ride but rarely these days?' inquired Mr Darcy after some moments of silence.

'I have not ridden once since the accident whose occurrence you so delightfully divined upon your first visit to my house. My old horse now enjoys the advantages of an honest day's labour on the farm, when not otherwise employed with the carriage. You are welcome to take a look at him. I have no doubt you could observe much of the creature's character and habits, or do your talents not extend to horses?'

'Do you shoot or fish?'

'No, I am quite a slave to my idleness, Mr Darcy. It affords me no leisure for the pursuit of the sports with which gentlemen generally occupy themselves in the country,' replied Mr Bennet.

Little did Mr Bennet like the tenor of Mr Darcy's questions and still less the scrutiny of which he had the misfortune to be the sole occupant. Though Mr Bennet's faults amounted to no more than a waste of the intellect and talents which he possessed, the folly of an imprudent marriage to a lady with excessive tastes in furnishings and dress, and an indulged fondness for port, he did not like to feel them exposed. His was a character more suited to finding amusement in the foolishness of others than to reflecting on his own shortcomings.

Fortunately, Mr Bennet was subjected to only a few minutes more of Mr Darcy's silent inspection of his person and house, and no further questions, before Elizabeth returned with a thick roll of paper secured with a red ribbon.

'I do believe that is everything you require, Mr Darcy.' Elizabeth handed the papers to Mr Darcy before sitting but as soon as he had them in possession, he rose to his feet.

'I thank you. I shall trespass on your time no longer. Good day, Mr Bennet, Miss Bennet.' Mr Darcy bowed curtly and headed for the door.

Elizabeth rose to follow him but he dismissed her with a wave of his hand. 'Pray, do not trouble yourself, Miss Bennet. I know the way.'

Elizabeth looked after him, curious at his abrupt departure and surprised that she regretted it.

9

The breakfast parlour at Longbourn had seldom witnessed such jubilation in the spirits of its mistress as it did the following morning.

'Mr Bennet,' began his wife, clutching a letter in her hand, 'I have just received an invitation to dine at Barton Park this very evening! What a wonderful thing for our girls.'

'I have no doubt that Lady Middleton will provide us with as fine a dinner as we might hope from any of our neighbours, but what is that to our girls? They none of them look malnourished.'

'Fie, Mr Bennet, why must you try my patience with such nonsense? I do not care at all for what Lady Middleton would feed them – but there are such opportunities available at such an occasion.'

'I should consider food the one source of delight that can be relied upon at a dinner and well worth the attention of any sensible girl,' said Mr Bennet, punctuating his remark with a large bite of sausage.

'I assure you, Father, that I shall give due attention to the dishes lain before me,' said Elizabeth with a smile, 'but I believe Mamma is referring to the agreeable conversations and society that such a dinner should provide. I am sure some of us must place the pleasures of such good company above all others.' She threw a teasing glance at Jane.

'Indeed, Lizzy, that is just what I think.' Mrs Bennet nodded and winked at Jane, who turned her eyes down to her plate. 'For you know Bingley will be there. Jane, you must apply some of Mr Perry's luminous powder when you dress tonight. It will hide your freckles and give your complexion such an agreeable glow. I have an idea it might reduce the impact your nose has upon your features, as well.'

Lydia whimpered at her mistress' feet to enquire after her own breakfast, and a chuckling Mrs Bennet scooped up the pug onto her lap. 'Do not worry, my dear. You shall not miss out on such an occasion. I am sure Lady Middleton extends the invitation to include you, for she most expressly said she hoped to have the pleasure of seeing *all* our family.' She fed Lydia half a sausage from her own plate.

'Lizzy, I would have you make the best of what attractions you possess. There is still hope for you, for you know Mr Darcy will be there. You should wear your Indian muslin, for you look less plain in that than anything else – and you may wear some of the luminous powder, too.'

'I thank you for the attentions, Mamma, but I have

not the least intention of dressing up in the ridiculous hope that it should entice a gentleman's attentions.'

'Indeed, I must agree with you, sister,' said Mary earnestly from the far side of the breakfast table. 'For vanity, we are told, is a deadly sin, and a lady's modesty is her true beauty.'

Elizabeth bit her lip to conceal a smirk. 'When faced with the unhappy choice of slathering myself in Mr Perry's concoctions or pleading modesty, I fear I must choose the latter. Mamma, you have raised a daughter who is too virtuous to make any effort to improve her appearance.'

'What nonsense, Lizzy! You could not be considered vain by anyone, I should think. A very pretty girl should take care not to appear conceited, but you have nothing to fear,' insisted Mrs Bennet. 'In any case, ensure you treat Mr Darcy with utmost civility. He paid you a great compliment in singling you out for a walk the other day.'

'I doubt you would consider it any great compliment if you had heard the manner of his conversation. Mr Darcy would never think to speak to me or any other lady, I imagine, if his investigation did not require it.'

'There will be no talk of that this evening, I assure you. I think it very wise of Sir John and Lady Middleton to arrange a dinner party, for no one would ruin a fine occasion with the discussion of such morbid matters.' Mrs Bennet smiled, too contented by the thought of the evening's entertainments to notice that Lydia had started licking her breakfast plate. 'And I insist upon you confining your remarks to suitable topics, Lizzy, and we'll have none of your pert remarks or contrariness, if you please.'

'I wonder that you allow me to attend at all if I am expected to neither look nor talk as myself,' muttered Elizabeth.

Mary produced her copy of Fordyce's Sermons and offered it to her sister. 'Indeed, a lady should school her manners and conversation, and it behoves us all to overcome those aspects of our nature which are neither virtuous nor agreeable. Does not Doctor Fordyce himself tell us that men of the best sense are averse to the thought of marrying a witty female?'

Elizabeth laughed and shook her head at the proffered book. 'Upon my word, why is everyone under the dreadful misapprehension that I should wish to win the attentions of Mr Darcy, of all people? I assure you that the prospect of becoming a spinster has never looked more agreeable to me than it does now.'

'There, there, Lizzy,' said her father with a smile. 'I would have you speak to Mr Darcy with as much wit and impertinence as you can muster for the occasion. How are we to enjoy such an evening if we are not to make sport amongst our neighbours?'

'Oh, Mr Bennet, will you not oblige me this once and insist upon your daughter attempting some degree of ladylike behaviour?' cried Mrs Bennet.

'I think this evening should be a very tedious affair if we were all obliged to sit mutely while Mr Darcy rattles off more of his impressive deductions about us all.' Mr Bennet dabbed his mouth and stood up from the table, hoping against all experience that this was the end of the matter.

The rest of the day in Longbourn was spent in considerable uproar, with Mrs Bennet's voluble insistence on the matters of Elizabeth's dress and conduct for the evening being met with resolute refusals. Jane willingly submitted to the excruciating winding of her hair into a mass of knotted curls. Her stays were fastened more tightly than either comfort or propriety would recommend, but it was the application of luminous powder to her face which caused the most distress, as Lydia found the phosphorescent substance's scent most appetising. The pug yapped and danced around as soon as Mrs Bennet loosened the lid of the tin.

'Lydia! Be quiet,' Mrs Bennet commanded, but the pug paid her no heed. She snapped and darted at the flecks that scattered in the air as Mrs Bennet dabbed a puff into the chalky powder.

Jane sneezed. 'Are you sure it is wise for me to wear the powder, Mamma? I fear it may induce me to cough and I should...'

Mrs Bennet smeared the powder puff over Jane's face and, seeing the pleasing glow in Jane's reflection in the looking glass, daubed the puff once more in the tin and patted another healthy dollop on Jane's nose. Jane spluttered as the powder flew up her nostrils.

'There you are, Jane. It hides your freckles well, does it not?' Mrs Bennet squeezed her daughter's shoulder and giggled. 'Mr Bingley is certain to fall in love with you now!'

Unfortunately, in this happy moment Mrs Bennet had carelessly lowered the hand holding the powder puff and Lydia jumped up to seized it. She ran about the room with the puff, growling and shaking it in her teeth, and coating herself in the luminous powder.

Elizabeth, who had heard the commotion from her chamber, rushed into the room. 'What is it?' She relaxed when she saw that the source of the disturbance was no more than Lydia's frenzied attack on a powder puff.

'No, Lydia. Drop that at once!' Mrs Bennet saw that her stern voice produced no effect on the dog, and tried a soft, coaxing tone. 'Lydia, darling, you have no need of the shiny powder. You already have such a lovely glossy coat. Give it to Mamma, darling.'

The pug shook the puff in her jaws with a savage determination.

'I do not think she will be prevailed upon to release it, Mamma,' laughed Elizabeth. 'I have not seen Lydia more fixed upon any target that was not dressed in regimentals.'

'Lydia, I insist upon you dropping that puff! Lydia! Drop it! Oh, you bad dog!'

Then, to the complete surprise of everyone in the room, most of all Lydia, Mrs Bennet whacked the pug on the nose. The shock of the blow forced the dog to drop the puff. She let out the most offended yelp before scampering out of the room.

Jane and Elizabeth looked at each other in astonishment as their mother bent down and picked up the puff, daubing it once more in the powder as though nothing had happened.

'Mamma, surely you do not intend to apply that to my face now?' Jane looked horrified.

'Why not? You are far too sallow. A young lady in love should have a healthy glow about her complexion.'

'But the dog has chewed it!'

'That is your fault. If you had not made such a fuss, then Lydia would not have got excited.'

Elizabeth interjected on her sister's behalf. 'I believe Jane's complexion boasts more than enough radiance to satisfy Mr Bingley of her improved health and esteem.'

Mrs Bennet turned to regard her second eldest. 'I suppose Jane looks well enough, but what of you, Lizzy? You cannot wear that gown. It is three years old at least, and how many times has Lady Middleton seen you in it? You look as though you have not slept in weeks. I suppose I must apply some powder to you, though you have done nothing to deserve such attention.'

'Indeed, I neither deserve nor wish for such attentions, I assure you,' replied Elizabeth. 'I am determined to dress as you see me now and there is no time to change. Consider how much fairer Jane will appear next her ill-looking sister.'

'Oh Lizzy, how you try my nerves! I insist upon you changing into your muslin, or you shall not attend the dinner at all.'

Thus began a heated exchange which lasted until the carriage was ready and waiting for them. Mrs Bennet had half a mind to lock both Lydia and Elizabeth in the closet beneath the stairs as punishment, but the pitiful whimpering of the former earned clemency for both and the entire Bennet family departed for Barton Park, the pug still with a shimmering muzzle and Elizabeth in her faded dress.

Lady Middleton looked every inch the resplendent peacock in a fine cerulean gown and jewelled feather headdress as she and her husband greeted their guests. She appeared most pleased with herself, as indeed she was. It had been a triumph of her ingenuity to persuade Mr Bingley it would be beneficial to Mr Woodhouse's spirits to dine at Barton Park, and if Mr Darcy disagreed with her declaration that conversing with witnesses over dinner was vastly more agreeable than dashing about the neighbourhood to interview them, he at least did not openly say so. Indeed he had not objected to the proposed dinner party at all.

Mr Woodhouse had been never been able to resist an invitation, although he had not dined out since his daughter's death. As Mr Woodhouse took the trouble to inform everyone present, and indeed some persons more than once, he had much better eat gruel than anything too rich, and he had only come because he knew he would be in the care of Mr Bingley.

Mr Darcy felt he might observe a great deal about the Bennets and Mr Woodhouse this evening, and was pleased that Lady Middleton had arranged the dinner. He correctly surmised that her motives for doing so were not altruistic – she was eager to know how his investigation proceeded and what he spoke of to her neighbours, for he had shared little of his inquiries with her. He suspected that Sir John made a habit of regaling her with tales of his cases and that she expected all gossip was owed to her as the magistrate's wife.

'Ah, Miss Bennet, I can see you are looking well.' Mr Bingley greeted Jane in the highest spirits and they enjoyed some happy moments of conversation before Mr Woodhouse required the doctor's consultation on whether he ought to be seated near the fire, or if there was a danger that too much warmth would exacerbate his nerves.

To Elizabeth's surprise, Mr Darcy not only greeted her with more than expected cordiality, but he thanked her for her drawings and complimented her skills.

'I hope they prove of some use to you, Mr Darcy,' she said, a little embarrassed that her heart should speed up at his praise, although of course such an elevation in pulse was only due to professional pride and not at all his handsome appearance in formal dinner attire. 'I set out only to sketch what I saw. I have no flair for art.'

'I am glad to hear it. You have an excellent forensic eye, one that sees the mundane details which many might overlook. The world is filled with obvious things which nobody observes, and yet these aspects are vital to the detective.'

Elizabeth nodded but before she could reply, Lady Middleton swept over.

'How lovely to see you, Elizabeth. You are looking very…' Lady Middleton's gaze swept over Elizabeth's old gown and plain hair. '…*animated* this evening. I do hope you have induced Darcy to share some news of his investigation. I have not seen him converse so openly with anyone but Bingley since he arrived.' She laughed and Elizabeth wondered that her words could so irritate Mr Darcy, yet Lady Middleton did not perceive it.

'I believe it is customary for detectives to seek information rather than reveal it,' replied Elizabeth.

'Indeed,' said Mr Darcy, as severe in tone and expression as ever. 'One should not mistake civility for candour.' He bowed his head stiffly and walked away to join Mr Woodhouse.

Lady Middleton raised an eyebrow. 'Nonetheless, I am convinced there is no need for this absolute secrecy with those of us who were friends of the victims. You must assist me, Elizabeth, in persuading Darcy that we are allies to his cause.'

'You overestimate my abilities. I have not yet convinced Mr Darcy to trust me as a witness; as for a confidante, I should think it impossible.'

'I have never known you to shrink from a challenge, Elizabeth. I had expected you to be as eager as anyone to discover what happened to your friends.'

Lady Middleton continued in this vein for a little while before the matter of observing to Mrs Bennet how well Jane looked, and how attentive Mr Bingley had been to her, proved a more promising source of gossip.

Elizabeth was not left without a companion for long. Harriet Smith approached her with a most nervous expression. 'I hope you will not be angry with me,' she began in a hushed voice, 'but I must tell you that I have informed Mr Darcy of what we did that day in the woods.'

'Of course I am not angry with you. You had every right to inform Mr Darcy of our actions and in any case, I should never have wished to keep it secret.'

Harriet smiled and grabbed Elizabeth's hand, pulling her aside so that they might converse in confidence. 'I am glad you feel so, for I do not think I could refuse Mr

Darcy anything, even if you did wish it.'

Elizabeth grinned and squeezed Harriet's hand. 'Be assured, my dear Harriet, that you have nothing to fear. I should never impose any secrecy on you or oblige you to withstand the interrogations of fearsome detectives. I hope Mr Darcy did not frighten you in his extraction of this intelligence.'

'Frighten me? Oh no. You do him an injustice to suggest such a thing, for he was most kind. Indeed when I asked him yesterday when he returned to Hartfield whether he thought I had behaved very badly, he said I had nothing to reproach myself for and that he believed I had been entirely honest with him.' Harriet beamed as though the merest recollection of these words was sufficient to induce perfect happiness.

'Well, that is high praise indeed from Mr Darcy,' said Elizabeth, though her arch tone and expression were not apprehended by her young companion.

Harriet's eyes brightened and she nodded with much enthusiasm. 'It is, is it not? Oh, Miss Elizabeth, I am so glad you agree, for it gives me to feel that perhaps I am worthy of such a compliment from him.'

'Of course you are, dear Harriet. I am sure you deserve far greater praise than that, and from more effusive gentlemen.'

'Oh no. I should not care for a compliment from any other man in the world. I believe I value no gentleman's judgement equal to Mr Darcy's, nor is there any other soul on earth whose admiration could matter more to me.'

'Harriet, you astonish me. What can Mr Darcy be

to you after so short an acquaintance, that you bestow such exultations upon him? You cannot have met him more than twice.'

'No, that is not the case at all.' Harriet shook her head, her blue eyes earnest. 'I have been so fortunate as to meet with Mr Darcy upon three separate occasions, if you count tonight. I must confess that I have developed so ardent an admiration for him that I can scarcely conceive of the strength of feeling that should arise from the fourth or fifth encounter.'

It was during this last heartfelt speech that Mrs Bennet drew closer to Harriet and Elizabeth. She held Lydia in her arms and edged towards the window as though she were enjoying the magnificent view of the park in the twilight, but her attention was all on the conversation behind her. There was something in Harriet's countenance that awakened a dark suspicion in her. She had always thought there was something artful about the Smith girl and no doubt she would do her utmost to snatch Bingley away from Jane. Could the wretched girl have won the good doctor's affection already? What other reason had she to confide in Elizabeth with such a besotted expression upon her face? Oh, how insupportable that Harriet Smith, who was no more than the natural of somebody, should succeed over one of her daughters! She moved closer to attend to their conversation.

'But Harriet, I do not think that it is wise to believe yourself in love,' said Elizabeth. 'Consider his purpose for coming to the neighbourhood. It is most likely he will return to London as soon as the investigation is brought to an end, and if Mr Darcy's talents are half as good as he and most of the world believe them to be, then he shall not be in the area very long at all. Certainly not long enough for a serious attachment to form, or for anything to arise from it.'

Mrs Bennet smiled at the unusual feeling of being pleased with her daughter. Surely Elizabeth felt that Mr Bingley's heart should belong to Jane, and was doing her best to persuade Harriet out of her plans to steal him.

'I suppose you think I am not worthy of so fine a gentleman,' replied Harriet. 'Maybe it is hopeless for me to dream of winning his affections, but I think it is most unkind of you to say so.'

'I did not mean to offend you. I am sure any gentleman would be honoured to have won your heart, but I cannot think it sensible to believe oneself in love with a man whom you know so little about.'

'I know that I shall never love another man as long as I live. Maybe it is not sensible or wise, but what is that to great love?'

Before Elizabeth could respond Sir John came over to talk with them and the matter was promptly dropped. However, neither Elizabeth nor Mrs Bennet could stop thinking about Harriet's declaration, and both of them watched her a great deal over dinner. Mr Darcy and Mr Bingley were seated across from Harriet with only Jane between them, so from the far end of the table, Elizabeth and Mrs Bennet could read the same meaning in Harriet's shy smiles whilst each believing that she directed them at a different gentleman.

Elizabeth could not understand it. She had known Harriet to be a meek and artless girl; not the smartest of creatures perhaps, but she had never thought her silly enough for such rash romantic sentimentality. It bothered her more than she felt it should. She knew she had offended Harriet and was sorry for it, but surely as a friend it was her duty to caution her against such foolishness. Mr Darcy never looked at any lady except to observe their faults. Even when Elizabeth detected him watching her over dinner, she was certain it was only to look for evidence of her guilt in the manner with which she held her fork.

Yet when she heard from Sir John that Mr Darcy had praised the honesty of Miss Smith and said that she had been of some assistance to him, she felt indignant. How did Harriet merit such praise when she, who had worked so tirelessly on the investigation, received only his censure and superior remarks? Perhaps Mr Darcy did feel some tenderness towards Harriet, for he could not consider that she had been of more assistance than Elizabeth unless he felt some partiality for the girl.

Mrs Bennet's anger at Harriet increased with every course – those doe-eyed expressions, the lowered lashes and simpering looks as she glanced across the table. For such a slight thing, of only sixteen years, she certainly knew how to make the most of her appearance. Mrs Bennet had never thought Harriet beautiful until that night, but when she beheld her laughing sweetly with shining blue eyes and auburn ringlets bouncing at her temples, her estimation of the girl's charm greatly increased.

That night, Harriet Smith unknowingly signed her death warrant.

10

Mrs Bennet had neither the time nor patience to carefully plan a method for dispatching Harriet Smith. She seized upon the opportunity afforded at Barton Park to invite the girl to visit them the following day, but that left little time for her to contemplate her next move.

Once the Bennets had gone to their beds, she set her mind to the task. She saw there might be considerable advantage if Harriet were to be killed during a visit to Longbourn, as that would lure Mr Darcy and his friend back to see the family, if only to question them. However, she felt it would be unwise to have the girl murdered on the property itself, lest suspicion should fall on one of the servants or worse still, Mr Bennet. If her husband were hanged for murder, both she and the girls would be turned out of their own home by the wretched cousin to whom the estate was entailed. No, that must not be allowed to happen. Harriet must be murdered close to Longbourn, but at some place where anybody might have been able to commit the deed.

The most propitious plan would be to attack Harriet as she walked to their house. This was a short journey and there would be no guarantee of privacy on the road, but there was something … thrilling in such a risk. All she needed was to devise an opportunity to get away unseen – but how might the mistress of Longbourn leave her home at the very time a guest was expected without raising suspicion among her family and servants?

Lydia, who lay beside her in bed, snored and rolled over in her sleep, her paws twitching and lips quivering as she dreamt of great chases. Of course! Dear, sweet, wonderful Lydia had inspired a solution.

The Bennets had barely quit the breakfast parlour the following morning when Mrs Bennet sounded the alarm.

'Hill, Hill!' she cried for her housekeeper as she ran through the great hall, flinging open the library door to invade her husband's solitude. 'Oh, Mr Bennet! You must come at once! Something dreadful has happened.'

Mr Bennet looked up in astonishment from his book. 'What is it, my dear? Has another family announced an engagement for one of their daughters?'

'Mr Bennet, how can you tease me at a time like this? I am speaking of my poor sweet Lydia.'

'Am I to understand, then, that Lydia is to be married?' said Mr Bennet, removing his glasses. 'I have often heard from you that she was a favourite among the officers. Has one of them returned to make her an offer?'

'Oh, Mr Bennet. There is no time for your nonsense. Lydia has gone missing and we must make haste if we are to find her,' replied his wife. The housekeeper had appeared discreetly by the doorway. 'Hill, Lydia has disappeared. You must see that all the servants go out and look for her. Who knows what could happen to my poor little darling out there all alone!'

'Yes, ma'am.' Hill curtsied and set off to follow her mistress' instructions before she could add any more, for when Mrs Bennet was vexed she had a tendency to demand half a dozen things be done all at once and then call for the smelling salts before the first task was completed.

Jane, followed by her sisters, hurried into the library. 'Mamma, whatever has happened?'

'Ah, there you are, girls, I must tell you most distressing news. This will come as a great shock for I know you all look on Lydia as a beloved sister.' Had Mrs Bennet noticed the look her daughters exchanged she would have attributed it to sibling jealousy owing to the fact that Lydia was far prettier than any of them. 'Lydia is missing! I let her into the garden some thirty minutes ago and she has not returned.'

Elizabeth sighed. 'Is that all? No doubt she is occupying herself with chasing a rabbit or some other creature. There is no cause for such alarm, Mamma. She will return when she is ready.'

'Oh, Lizzy! How can you talk so coldly when you know Lydia is a good girl and would never run off like that? No, something terrible must have happened for she is not the sort of pug to do that sort of thing and you must all go out and search for her.'

Elizabeth refrained from informing her mother that she thought it very likely it had only been the prospect of sport or food that had enticed Lydia to scamper off over the countryside. However, as pointless as searching for an absconding pug seemed, it might afford an opportunity for more interesting inquiries or, at the very least, some exercise. 'Perhaps Jane and I should go and ask at the neighbouring farms. They may have seen her there.'

'Yes, yes, you must go at once,' said Mrs Bennet, waving her lace handkerchief at them before raising it to dab at her eyes. 'And Mr Bennet, you must take Mary and Kitty and search the grounds for her. Perhaps she has got caught in the hedgerows! Oh, my poor Lydia! What if she is hurt? Oh, Mr Bennet. How can you sit there still? You must go and look for her. Make haste, make haste.'

Mr Bennet considered his options. It was true that he was not prodigiously fond of exercise but when faced with the alternative of an increasingly shrill wife in hysterics, a stroll about the garden appeared quite agreeable. 'Come now, Mary, Kitty. I believe we would be best to do as your mother says. I shan't bear the pug any ill will if she has the good grace to be found near the house and does not require any strenuous activity in her rescue.'

Mrs Bennet hurried her family out of Longbourn, instructing them to call Lydia in a tone not too severe, lest it distress her delicate sensibilities, but with enough urgency to provoke the pug's immediate return. By the time her husband and daughters had set out, she was quite out of breath. It was a testament to her resolve that she wasted not one moment before calling out once more: 'Hill, Hill! Where are my smelling salts? I am so vexed by this dreadful business I am sure I shall faint if you do not come.'

Hill hurried back into the great hall to see her mistress at the foot of the staircase, clutching at the carved end of the balustrade. 'Shall I help you to your bedchamber, ma'am?'

'Yes, I shall go to my room, for I do not think I have the strength to stand. I shall take no comfort or rest there, though. I suffer such terrible beatings at my heart and spasms of my nerves.'

Thus Mrs Bennet was helped to her room. To Hill's surprise she was not then instructed to fetch cups of sugary tea or a glass of Madeira to ease her mistress' nerves but rather urged to go and search for Lydia, for Mrs Bennet informed her she would feel no benefit from any restorative until her poor sweet pug was returned to her.

Once Mrs Bennet heard Hill's footsteps recede down the stairs she leapt from her bed and went to the window to watch the servant head out into the garden below to join the search. Quickly, she went to her closet. She would have no time to change into her husband's old clothes as she had for the other murders, but it was very unlikely that anyone should see her in any case. With three successful murders behind her, Mrs Bennet was surely too accomplished to worry about such things.

'There, there, Lydia, my love,' whispered Mrs Bennet at the closet door. Loud scratching and snuffling noises emerged from the other side of the closet door, followed by a piteous whimper. 'Not much longer now, my sweet.'

The whimpering grew louder and Mrs Bennet, cooing comforting words to her pug, opened the door a few inches. A lurid glow sprang forward from the bottom of the dark closet and startled Mrs Bennet before she realised the unnatural light was nothing more than Lydia's luminescent muzzle. The pug had happened upon the tin of phosphorescent powder and it appeared she had occupied herself with licking and nibbling at it whilst confined within the closet. The excessive amount of saliva this activity stimulated reacted with the powder to create a slather of discoloured froth about her jaws and cheeks. The effect was not a flattering one.

'Oh, Lydia! You look a fright,' Mrs Bennet scolded the pug before taking her dark green walking cloak from the closet and going to shut the door. Lydia, not enthusiastic about once more being shut in the closet, lunged at the opening. Mrs Bennet had not the time to persuade Lydia of the necessity of her re-incarceration, and she slammed the closet door shut.

Had Mrs Bennet been in less of a hurry she might have noticed that the pug had stuck out her paw, and that the loud yelp when she shut the closet was the result of the door slamming on her foot. Thus Mrs Bennet snuck out of Longbourn without realising that an excited pug was limping not far behind her.

Mrs Bennet's heart pounded as she hurried down the road. Now that she was out of her home the fear of discovery was immense, for if but one person spotted her, it would put an end to her plan to eliminate the Smith girl. Fortunately, she did not encounter anyone on the open road, and she soon found herself in the shelter of overhanging branches as the path wound its way into the woodland.

She concealed herself behind the thick, knotted trunk of an old oak tree not six feet from the path and waited. Lydia, who was agile enough to scamper even with a limp, hurried after her mistress and yapped at her heel.

'Oh, Lydia. Whatever are you doing here?' admonished Mrs Bennet in hushed tones. 'You must be very still and quiet, for that wretched girl will come along here shortly.'

Lydia was, as her mistress had observed on numerous occasions, a pug of great beauty, refinement, and accomplishments. The capacity to remain still and quiet, however, was not among her blessings, least of all when she had been greatly excited by the consumption of phosphorescent powder and a period of confinement. Thus her reply to Mrs Bennet was a succession of enthusiastic barks.

'Hush!' scolded Mrs Bennet. 'Be quiet. You do not wish to scare off that little baggage, do you?'

'Rrrofff?' Lydia tilted her head, her jaws gleaming with drool. She contemplated her mistress' stern expression for a moment before becoming so overwhelmed with excitement that she could not suppress an outburst of exhilarated yaps.

Happily, the necessity to wait was not prolonged and after only a few minutes of Mrs Bennet's failed attempts to persuade Lydia that silence was greatly to be desired, they heard dainty footsteps approaching.

'Stay,' commanded Mrs Bennet.

Lydia, in her animated state, assumed that she had been given leave to do something. Therefore she bounded out from behind the tree at great speed and headed for Harriet, flecks of luminous slobber flying off her delicate jowls.

Harriet, a warm-hearted girl who was fond of all creatures, bent down and held out her hands to the pug. 'Oh, you poor thing. What's happened to you?'

Mrs Bennet watched as Lydia licked the proffered hands. Clever Lydia, Mrs Bennet realised, had made it most easy for her to sneak behind the distracted girl. How delightfully easy it was to close in on her victim as she crouched down to pat the pug. Mrs Bennet reached down from behind and wrapped her hands around Harriet's slender throat. The wretched girl emitted a choked gasp but, already overbalanced from tending to Lydia, had not the strength to turn or fight against Mrs Bennet's iron grasp. Harriet kicked her heels against the road. She clawed at the hands clutching her throat, but to no avail. The deed was done.

Lydia looked up at her mistress, uncertain of the next stage in the game. She had enjoyed watching the struggle, although Harriet's flailing arms and legs had required her to dart some distance back for fear of being kicked, but Harriet had gone quite limp now and did not stir when Lydia snatched a mouthful of the girl's dress and shook it in her jaws.

'Leave that, Lydia, dear,' said Mrs Bennet, her eyes bright from her exertions. 'There's no time to play.'

She dragged the unfortunate corpse to the side of

the road. She had wished to take it further but the dead weight of even a small girl proved too much and she dared not take too long.

'Let us hurry home, my sweet,' said Mrs Bennet. 'We must get you clean, and then you shall go to the garden to be found. It will do Mr Bennet's spirits good to rescue you, I am sure.'

They left the body to await discovery and hurried back to Longbourn to resume their expected roles. Mrs Bennet hoped the rescue of Lydia might be fully played out long before the dead girl was found, and that there would be no call to delay the luncheon meal, for she was uncommonly hungry now.

11

The rest of the morning progressed in accordance with Mrs Bennet's plans; a fact which, in her estimation, owed more to her quick thinking and resourcefulness than any degree of good fortune. She returned to Longbourn without discovery and, after some slight regret that she must sacrifice a good lace handkerchief to clean Lydia's muzzle, persuaded the pug to run around the side of the house by throwing a stick in that direction. Lydia bounded after the wooden missile and, after an enjoyable minute of chomping, trotted back to the front door of Longbourn only to discover that her mistress had disappeared inside. She scratched and whimpered at the door, and when this activity yielded no success, trotted back into the garden.

Mrs Bennet hurried to her bedchamber, removed her cloak, and she had not been five minutes in her winged armchair posed in an attitude of great distress before she heard a clamour of footsteps upon the stairs.

A knock at her door scarcely preceded its opening and a beaming Mr Bennet walked in, holding an excited pug and followed by his two younger daughters. 'There you are, Mrs Bennet, we have found Lydia for you. I think we may boast that we are in possession of one of the silliest dogs in England for the little thing bounded up to us in the shrubbery, happy as you please, with no thought of the distress or inconvenience she had caused.'

He lowered the dog to the floor, tousled her head with half-hearted affection, and rubbed his hands as he stood back up. As soon as she was released, Lydia scampered over to Mrs Bennet, jumped up on her lap and licked her face in a convincing performance of a dog reunited with its mistress after a lengthy separation.

'Oh my dear Lydia!' cried Mrs Bennet. There was no need for her to feign happiness, for all her schemes had been realised to perfection.

'It was I who saw her first, Mamma,' said Kitty, eager to claim her share of the credit. 'I told Father that I saw something approaching through the hedges, did I not?'

'I believe I mentioned that I had heard something that sounded very much like Lydia long before you saw anything,' insisted Mary.

'Oh, that is not fair. You know it was I who spotted her first.'

'I know nothing of the kind, and I think that—'

'Girls, girls,' interrupted Mr Bennet. 'Let us satisfy ourselves that both Kitty's eyes and Mary's ears were of invaluable service in the apprehension of the pug. If I had thought the dog's rescue could no more bring peace to the house than her disappearance, I should have left her to wander for weeks.'

'Oh, Mr Bennet, how could you say such a thing? Leave poor Lydia outside? An insufferable notion!' Mrs Bennet wagged her finger but the smile had not left her face. She stood up with Lydia in her arms and ushered her family from the room. 'Now, I must call for Hill and tell her the search is at an end. There is much to be done this morning.'

'Indeed, my dear. The cook must return to the kitchen, or I fear greatly for our luncheon. I am, as a rule, not a man who enjoys delays in the prandial schedule and I find that the excitement of the morning has greatly increased my appetite and need for sustenance.'

Mrs Bennet hurried herself about, informing the household that the search had yielded a most happy result. All were much relieved, with the exception of Jane and Elizabeth, who were too far afield to be informed. It was over an hour before the two eldest Miss Bennets traipsed back to their home, Elizabeth having finally persuaded Jane that the pug was not likely to be found by further exertion on their part and would as likely as not return of her own accord.

'Lydia has been found!' exclaimed Jane upon entering the drawing room, beholding the pug contentedly lolling about on the rug by Mrs Bennet's feet. 'How wonderful! What a comfort that must have been to you, Mamma.'

'I wonder that after so much trouble was taken in the search for Lydia, no one thought to do half as much to inform Jane or me of its conclusion,' said Elizabeth as she sat down and regarded her family arranged in their usual activities. 'Where is Harriet? Has she not come?'

'Harriet? Gracious, I forgot her visit in all this morning's distress,' replied Mrs Bennet. 'Perhaps she has decided not to come, or has been waylaid by her aunt.'

Elizabeth frowned and shook her head. 'Harriet would never abandon an engagement without explanation. Perhaps we should go look for her?'

'I see no cause for that,' said her mother. 'Heavens, Lizzy, can you not sit still for two minutes without imagining some reason to set off again? No, you will stay here and have lunch with your family. If Harriet has not come by the end, you may walk out to fetch her if you please, although I dare say she will not thank you for your efforts if she has simply forgotten or changed her mind.'

'I do not think I should feel easy until I know that Harriet is either here or has called again at Hartfield,' replied Elizabeth. 'Consider that there is a murderer abroad who has struck three times and could strike again.'

'All the more reason for you to stay at home. You will not disoblige me in this, or you shall never set foot out of this house again.'

'Come now, Lizzy,' said Mr Bennet, 'there is no danger in taking a little lunch before you set off. I wager a mislaid house guest is a good deal easier to find than an absconding pug, and far more likely to turn up of her own accord in due time. You need not fear any evil should befall Harriet as I doubt our local villain would be brazen enough to act with Mr Sherlock Darcy in the neighbourhood.'

Elizabeth acquiesced to her father's wishes, but her anxieties were by no means allayed. All through the luncheon meal she could not attend to her family's conversation, nor could she quiet her mind's fear for Harriet. At every sound she looked to the door, hoping for her friend's arrival, but when Hill entered at the completion of the Bennets' meal it was to announce the arrival of Mr Darcy and Mr Bingley.

Mrs Bennet's eyes lit up. She had not flattered herself that her efforts would be rewarded with such alacrity. 'We shall receive them in the drawing room,' she told Hill before returning her attention to her eldest. 'Oh, Jane! Why did you wear that dress on today of all days? It is most plain. You must go change. No, there is not time. Just pinch your cheeks and try not to slouch so. Come now, girls. Make haste. We must not keep the gentlemen waiting.'

Thus the Bennets were led into the drawing room by a bustling mother who, like the most conscientious of colonels, led her troops from the front.

When the bows and curtseys had been made, Bingley looked apologetically at the Bennets, though Mrs Bennet was convinced his eyes rested longer on Jane than any other. 'We are very sorry to intrude on you like this, and it grieves me that our visit to your home shall bring you much pain. Yet we have to inform you of the most shocking and dreadful news,' said he. 'Perhaps, Mr Bennet, you might consider it better that we should speak to you alone on this matter?'

'No, indeed,' replied Mr Bennet, sitting down in his chair. 'If there is bad news to be delivered, let you be the messenger of it to us all.'

Mrs Bennet sat down and motioned for the girls to do the same, which Lydia understood as permission to position herself upon Mrs Bennet's lap. Only Darcy and Bingley remained standing.

'Well, Mr Bingley. We are ready to receive your news, as you see.' Mrs Bennet nodded at him and took a deep breath, preparing to give a convincing performance as a lady stricken with shock and grief.

Bingley looked most uncomfortable and Mr Darcy, moved by equal parts impatience and a desire to spare his friend from further uneasiness, took over the role of bearer of bad tidings.

'We have come here to inform you that Miss Harriet Smith was discovered dead at ten past eleven this very morning,' said Mr Darcy. 'We have reason to believe from Mrs Goddard that she had set out in the hopes of visiting you here at Longbourn.'

'No, no, it cannot be,' Jane stammered, pale with disbelief.

'Poor Harriet,' whispered Elizabeth. She took Jane's hand and squeezed it, biting her lip to stop herself from crying, not from shock, but from the worse blow that her growing dread had become most brutally realised.

Kitty, who was the same age as Harriet, burst into tears, and Mary clasped the small cross she wore.

Mrs Bennet, not to be outdone by her daughters, commenced crying at once and augmented her excessively loud sobbing with dramatic gesticulations with her handkerchief. Lydia tried to provide comfort by snapping at the handkerchief, persuaded that it was the source of her mistress' distress. Mr Bennet looked shocked and saddened but said nothing.

Bingley could not have looked guiltier if he had been personally responsible for the latest murder. 'I am so sorry to have brought such ill news into your house, Mr Bennet. We shall leave you now but I fear we must return later to ask some questions, if you will allow.'

At this, Mrs Bennet ceased her tears at once. The gentlemen leave so soon? No, that would not do at all. But Elizabeth had observed the impatient expression on Mr Darcy's face and spoke before her mother was required to take action.

'There is no need to delay, at least not on my behalf,' said Elizabeth. 'I know full well that time alone is an insufficient palliative for the grief and loss of a murdered friend. I believe I should feel better if I knew I had done everything in my power to hasten the discovery of the villain responsible as soon as may be.'

'What Elizabeth means to say is that of course you must stay and talk to us. I believe you will find no one in the county who knew Harriet better than my daughters, for they were all excessively fond of her,' explained Mrs Bennet. 'They are such obliging girls, though I say so myself, that I am sure they all wish to do everything they can to aid your investigation. Is that not so, Jane?'

Jane blinked back tears as her mother nodded at her. 'Oh, yes, of course. I would not have you defer your questions on my account.'

'Then it is settled. We shall begin at once.' Mr Darcy clapped his hands.

'Indeed, and you must stay at Longbourn as long as

you like,' Mrs Bennet went on, 'I insist upon you dining with us tonight, for I am sure your investigations here shall take a good deal of the afternoon.'

'You are too kind and generous to think of us at a time such as this, Mrs Bennet,' said Mr Bingley. 'If it is no imposition upon you or your family, I believe we should gladly stay.' He threw a nervous glance at his friend, but no objection came. Mr Darcy stood silent, canvassing the Bennet faces.

'Perhaps I might volunteer to answer your questions first, Mr Darcy.' Elizabeth stood up. 'I hope it falls within your own requirements if I suggest that we conduct the interview whilst walking out in the gardens. You would not wish for my answers to prejudice my sisters' opinions and recollections, and I fear this may only be achieved through a private interview.'

Mrs Bennet wondered at her daughter's brazen impertinence in daring to instruct Mr Darcy in how to conduct his work. She felt certain that this wilful trait must be some defect in the Bennet line, for she was adamant that such sauciness was none of her influence. However, it seemed that Mr Darcy took no offence at Elizabeth's presumption.

'An apposite suggestion, and one I should wish to act upon without delay.' Mr Darcy started across the room to join Elizabeth, and paused by Mrs Bennet. He looked down at Lydia, reaching his hand out to hold her chin. 'An excellent specimen. Most refined features.' He patted the pug on the head and traced both his hands down behind her ears and along her cheeks. 'A near perfect descendent of a very fine breeding line, I should think.

Yes, a truly remarkable creature.'

'She is indeed, Mr Darcy. Lydia is admired wherever she goes,' Mrs Bennet informed him, feeling very proud that at least one of her girls had made a conquest of this aloof gentleman.

Lydia was also pleased with Mr Darcy's attentions and it was all Mrs Bennet could do to prevent the little pug from running after him when he left with Elizabeth. Bingley himself did not stay seated long before rising and asking Jane to accompany him out of doors where she might get some air, although not before he had once more apologised to the Bennets for having brought such unhappiness to their household, and assured Jane that he was unfit for the task of interviewing her. He could offer nothing but the diversion of conversation that, he hoped, would prove not entirely disagreeable to her.

12

Elizabeth and Darcy's conversation commenced as soon as they set foot upon the green lawn and, as both parties claimed the role of interrogator, the interview was by no means lacking in animation.

'What happened, Mr Darcy? Where was poor Harriet attacked and what was the manner of her death?'

'I cannot confess any surprise, Miss Bennet, that despite your avowed intention to answer my questions, you expect first to satisfy your own,' remarked Mr Darcy. 'You will not find me disobliging in this matter as there is no reason to conceal the facts: Miss Smith was found not far off the road about a quarter of a mile north from Longbourn. The cause of death appeared to be strangulation.'

'So close? I had not imagined it would be so near. Oh, poor Harriet. If only…' Elizabeth's voice faded as she redirected her thoughts. There was no use in reproaching herself for what she might have done if she had known.

She must concentrate on the facts. 'I suppose at least in this case there can be no doubt in anyone's mind that she was murdered.'

'No, there is no doubt.' They walked a few steps together in silence and it seemed dreadful to Elizabeth that the gardens should look so fair and that the sun should shine at such a time as this.

'Has Harriet been moved since the crime was discovered?' she asked. 'I believe I should be able to capture the scene most faithfully if I were permitted to see her *in situ*.'

'As Bingley and I have already attended the scene there is no need for you to draw it, Miss Bennet. I should benefit more from an account of the events of this morning from your point of view.'

Elizabeth shrugged. 'I fear there is little use in what I can tell you. My mother's pug, Lydia, went missing this morning and the household was set to searching for the ridiculous creature. Jane and I had the task of walking to the neighbouring farms to inquire after the dog.'

'So all your family and the servants were engaged in this search?'

'Indeed. My father came here with Mary and Kitty to look for her in the gardens and shrubbery, and the servants were sent to search in the stables and grounds.'

'And your mother?'

'She was too greatly distressed by Lydia's disappearance to be of any practical use. Mamma took to her bed for the duration, I believe.' Elizabeth frowned. 'The whole venture is grotesquely absurd in light of what happened to poor Harriet.'

'Not in the least. It may prove useful.' He stopped as they neared the end of the formal garden and turned to look at her. 'You must tell me the precise times and names of the individuals to whom you spoke.'

Elizabeth wondered if they should turn back, or redirect their walk to the avenue, but instead she started through the copse, beyond which lay no well-maintained garden, only the ill-tended parklands. She informed Mr Darcy of the particulars of her morning excursions as they traipsed through the trees and he walked beside her, offering no interruptions or remarks until she had finished.

'Excellent! Then there is no possibility that you or your sister could have been back to the road in time to have committed the crime. You have gained a sound alibi, and I am most gratified.'

'I wonder that you can speak so lightly of the event so soon. It is most unfeeling. How can poor Harriet's death mean so little to you?'

'A detective cannot afford to think sentimentally, Miss Bennet. A victim is better served by a first-rate investigation than any affectation of mourning from one whose attention must focus on the facts alone.'

'I can understand the purpose of such detachment when the victim is a stranger, but Harriet was by no means unknown to you. She did her best to help your investigations and admired you greatly, I believe. She would not wish her death to be so coldly dismissed by you as no more than a means to eliminate one, or perhaps two, suspects.'

'Perhaps not, but neither would she have wished for

any hindrance in the investigation. She was a singularly artless girl who did everything in her power to help seek justice for her cousin. You do her a discredit to remember her otherwise.'

Elizabeth looked sideways at him. The overhanging branches cast spindly shadows across his face and his stern features were more inscrutable to her than ever. 'Perhaps you possess a better appreciation of Harriet's qualities than I thought. I shall endeavour to focus my attentions on the case dispassionately – for her sake.'

'You had better give up your attempts to investigate altogether, Miss Bennet. I do not deny that you possess some talent, but you are too intimately connected with the case to be objective.'

'A desire for justice and sympathy for the victims are by no means incompatible.'

'Perhaps not, Miss Bennet, but the same sentiments you feel for the victims may also connect you with their killer.' His voice softened, although strangely it seemed more forceful, more determined. 'I would urge you, for what I hope to be the last time, to give up any further investigation into these deaths. I do not speak now from a desire to prevent you from complicating my enquiries, nor do I suspect you of any involvement in these crimes. However laudable your endeavours to find justice for your friends should be, I fear nothing can be gained from them but further grief and distress. I would have you quit for your own sake alone.'

'How could I possibly quit now Harriet has been killed? I shall do everything in my power to discover who is responsible and my actions will not be dictated by any other than my own thoughts and conscience. I had hoped you might now allow me to be of some assistance to your investigation.' She tilted her head with a most exaggerated expression of aloof indifference as they walked from the shaded grove to look out over sunlit fields. 'There, Mr Darcy. I can affect a manner of cold dispassion. Will that be enough to satisfy you that I am equal to the task?'

'Mimicry affords no better mask than wit, Miss Bennet. You conceal less than you think and you feel too greatly in this case.'

'With such powers of perception it is a very great wonder that you have not discovered the culprit of these crimes already,' retorted Elizabeth.

'Indeed, Miss Bennet, I should have solved this case before now! My failings in this are insupportable; that the murderer should have had time to claim another victim, and that Miss Smith has died owing to my negligence, is unpardonable.' Though the violent reproach in Mr Darcy's speech was directed at himself it seemed the surrounding landscape bore the brunt of his displeasure; he snapped off a nearby branch and decapitated several bluebells and dandelions, and Elizabeth feared that had a sheep foolishly wandered near, it might have received a good kicking.

'Mr Darcy, I spoke rashly and did not mean to imply that I or any other could find fault in your investigation or abilities,' she assured him. 'No one could blame you and indeed I am in no position to expect haste from anyone. I have thought of nothing but these murders for weeks and yet I have discovered so little.'

'You should not reproach yourself in this. No one

asked or expected you to investigate this case. However slow you find your progress, no one has depended on it. You have disappointed no one's expectations.'

'No; no one except myself. I suppose you think it abominably conceited that I should consider myself worthy to the task but I had much rather try and fail than to sit idly and do nothing.'

'Indeed, I do not consider it conceited at all. No detective admitted to the privilege of hearing your thoughts on the case could think them less than perceptive, Miss Bennet.' He looked at her with such warmth of admiration that though she was astonished, she could not doubt his sincerity. 'Never before I have encountered a lady who has taken on so much active involvement in an investigation. Nor have I known any amateur who has applied their talents so aptly to the discipline of forensic observation or possessed the astute intellect to deduce the pertinent facts.'

Elizabeth smiled. She felt so deeply moved and gratified by his compliments that she knew not how to make light of them. 'I confess I have had the benefit of instruction from reading Mr Bingley's published accounts of your cases. I believe I may have learnt a little of your methods from them.'

'After reading Bingley's fulsome portrayal of my abilities, I fear you must be disappointed in my progress.'

'Not at all. From what little I have been permitted to see of your investigation here, I should say his panegyrics of your expertise are by no means unfounded.'

At this Elizabeth thought she detected a smile flickering across his face; but then he turned and, with his usual stern countenance, indicated that they should make their way back through the copse. 'I know better than to openly accuse you of flattery, Miss Bennet, but I shall not be induced to involve you further in my investigation.'

Elizabeth, a little confused and, perhaps, more than a little offended at this cooling in his manner, soon rallied to counter his cold rebuff with a suitably arch response. 'Heaven forbid that I should presume such a privilege! Though I may no longer be thought of as a suspect, it would not do at all for the investigation to benefit from a collaboration of your experience and my local knowledge. How much lesser a triumph would the resolution of the case be to the great Mr Sherlock Darcy if any share of the credit were owed to another.'

'You speak too lightly, Miss Bennet, but let me assure you that credit means little to me and the conclusion of this case will bring more grief than satisfaction. I would that circumstances were different – that I could welcome your investigative efforts – but I cannot allow it.' He broke off and, as agitated as he sounded, Elizabeth was beginning to suspect he was repressing a good deal of his feelings on the matter when he continued in a calmer tone: 'Miss Bennet, I believe that the culprit will be connected to you; possibly very intimately connected.'

Elizabeth turned to question him but he fixed his gaze ahead and continued before she could make any enquiry. 'Every particular of the case informs me that the murderer must be local and well acquainted with the habits of their victims. For all that you suffer for your murdered friends, would not the knowledge that your efforts in the investigation brought another of your intimates to the gallows be greater still?'

'You are mistaken, Mr Darcy, if you think the pain I should feel at the demise of the murderer could equal any grief I should feel for the victims. The culprit's actions alone would be responsible for their downfall, not the discovery of their guilt; and I would have no regret at their capture.'

They had reached the edge of the copse and found themselves in the sunny garden once more. Jane and Mr Bingley were some distance ahead, sitting on a slat bench by the rose gardens. They each looked so serene and content in their conversation as to form a portrait the exact opposite of Mr Darcy's current feelings. 'It is easy to speak with such conviction when the murderer is no more than a hypothetical figure in the shadows, but even if you did feel as you say, what of your friends and family? Would they not blame you if you played a part in the apprehension and execution of one of their own?'

'I have never sought the gratitude of the neighbourhood, nor any praise for my efforts. I wish the murderer caught, and that is all,' said Elizabeth. 'If my involvement in the investigation should mean I was no longer welcome in any of the Hertfordshire houses, I should consider it a very small price to pay for the justice of four murdered friends and the restoration of safety to the neighbourhood.'

'Then you would not always wish to remain at Longbourn, I think? You believe your happiness would be found settled elsewhere?'

Elizabeth knew not what he meant by this remark, nor what he had inferred from her declaration. It took her some moments before she could reply. 'Mr Darcy, I cannot think of anything beyond this case, least of all my own happiness. I have every intention of continuing to investigate these murders, and I shall use any resources or powers I possess to hasten its conclusion. I would never reproach myself, nor you, nor any other detective who brought justice for these most despicable crimes.'

'A fine sentiment, but such absolutes are easily asserted in hypothetical circumstances.' He looked at her briefly before turning his gaze towards Longbourn in the distance. 'I fear there is little to be gained in continuing this discussion. I cannot do or say more at present, but I pray you will remember at the conclusion of this investigation that I did my best to dissuade you.'

He bowed curtly, took his leave and then marched back to the house, leaving a most perplexed Elizabeth. As baffling as the mystery was, she was certain that she had more hope of discovering the identity of the murderer than of ever understanding Mr Darcy.

13

While the announcement of Miss Harriet Smith's murder had caused Mrs Bennet neither shock nor grief, it had been followed by two most vexatious realisations: firstly, that Mr Darcy's interrogations at Longbourn should occupy most of the afternoon; and secondly, that his investigations would afford the family nothing more than inconvenience. Mr Bennet's library had been commandeered as the detective's private interview room; Mr Bingley had been sequestered to assist his friend; and so the Bennets were quite abandoned to themselves. Mr Darcy had even gone so far as to station their own footman to guard the front door of Longbourn for the family's protection, obliging them all to remain at home.

'I certainly had not imagined that to have one's house the centre of an investigation should be quite such a tedious affair,' said Mrs Bennet to her family. While her husband and daughters attempted to occupy themselves with their usual activities of reading or needlework, she could not attend to any such diversion. After all her daring and ingenuity in killing Harriet, it was intolerable to be so excluded from the investigative proceedings. Not even stroking the beloved pug on her lap afforded her any comfort or eased her agitation. 'To think that we should be told to remain in our sitting room, to be treated like captives in our own home, and await our summons from Mr Darcy.'

'An enforced and idle confinement is no cure for distress,' agreed Elizabeth. She set down her book. She had spent the last minutes tracing on its cover the route Harriet must have taken to Longbourn, and the many byways which intersected with the road and places where her murderer may have hidden. 'One had much rather be active and useful after such a tragedy, but we are witnesses and as such we must accede to the demands of Mr Darcy's investigation until we have all done our duty and divulged all we know.'

'I did not mind waiting before my interview and I do not mind waiting now after it. Patience, it is often said, is a virtue,' added Mary helpfully.

'Oh, hush, Mary,' snapped Mrs Bennet. 'You have been happy to wait because you have nothing better to do, and you were happier still to tell Mr Darcy all your thoughts because no one else would care to listen to them.'

'I should bear the waiting a good deal better in peace than with incessant prattle,' remarked Mr Bennet without looking up from his book.

'I am sure it will not be long until they require an interview with you, Mamma,' said Jane. 'Kitty cannot have much to tell them that they have not already heard from Mary. You will feel more at ease when you have been permitted to give your account of the morning.'

Elizabeth glanced at her sister. Poor Jane had scarcely recovered from the shock. Since Mr Bingley had left her side she had been much occupied in trying to comfort her mother and youngest sister.

'I am sure I know nothing that should make me anxious to speak with them, Jane,' replied Mrs Bennet, making her indignation most apparent. 'And I think it most improper that they should wish to speak to my daughters before me. I am mistress of Longbourn, after all. They should have desired my account first, if not for their own sense of propriety then out of consideration for my poor nerves, for I have suffered a most vexatious day.'

'You speak as though propriety or nerves hold any weight when balanced against the needs of a murder enquiry,' said Elizabeth. 'Remember, Mamma, that poor Harriet was killed this very day. You cannot expect Mr Darcy to stand on ceremony at a time such as this.'

'I do not need my own daughter to remind me of what distress I have endured this day. How could you speak so coldly to your own mother? That I had scarcely recovered from the most upsetting loss of my beloved Lydia before the dreadful news about that poor girl was forced upon me in my own home! Oh, it is too much to be borne.'

Mrs Bennet erupted into a display of sobs and cries with expert precision, eliciting awkward looks from her husband, earnest reassurances from Jane, and enthusiastic licks from her pug. Elizabeth was mortified that her mother could see so little reason at a time when it was most needed. How could she think only of herself and her own suffering when Harriet was dead? Let alone compare the grief of temporarily misplacing her dog with the brutal murder of their friend!

The door opened and Kitty stepped into the room. 'Mr Darcy asks if you would see him and Mr Bingley now, Father.'

Mrs Bennet looked up from her handkerchief. 'And now Mr Bennet is called before me as well? Oh, it is too much! My poor nerves will be shreds by the time they wish to see me – or perhaps they do not intend to speak to me at all, although I am the mistress of this house.'

Elizabeth seethed inwardly as Mrs Bennet burst into tears once more.

'Sorry, Mamma.' Kitty tiptoed over to her usual seat by Mary. 'I was just repeating what Mr Darcy said to…'

'Oh, hang what Mr Darcy said, Kitty! Can you not see the state I am in? Would you try my nerves further with your unfeeling explanations?'

'Calm down, my dear.' Mr Bennet rose to his feet and patted his wife's shoulder. 'I shall do as I am bid and speak with Mr Darcy now. I do not foresee the interview being of long duration, and I am sure you will soon have the opportunity to exhibit your grief before our guests.'

He quit the room with neither great haste nor reluctance, for the only pleasure he anticipated in the interview was the temporary absence from his wife's histrionics and complaints.

Some time after Mr Bennet had departed, Mrs Bennet's

need to converse won over her desire to impress upon her family the great distress she felt at all this business. 'I suppose you will no more oblige me with an account of what to expect than your sisters,' she muttered to Kitty.

'Mr Darcy made me swear not to discuss the matter with anyone until all of the household have been interviewed,' Kitty replied.

'Indeed Mamma, as you have already heard from each of us in turn, we have been instructed not to speak about the matter amongst ourselves,' Elizabeth reminded her. 'I believe Mr Darcy wants our accounts to be as untarnished as possible. Memories are apparently very susceptible beasts, prone to imagine they actually saw things that they heard another describe.'

'Fie, what nonsense! You may believe what you like of Mr Darcy's theories, Lizzy, but I think it nothing more than a means of tormenting us further. Is it not natural that a family should seek the solace of conversation after such an event? To impose such unfilial silence between a mother and her daughters in such distressing circumstances is most hard hearted.'

'It is a temporary imposition from which we suffer little discomfort. If he was as hard-hearted as you say, we might have been separated to await our interviews in isolation,' said Elizabeth, somewhat surprised to hear herself describing Mr Darcy's actions as a kindness. Indeed she had not regarded them as such until her mother had provoked her to defend them. She was about to furnish her family with further evidence that they had been treated with comparative generosity by relating a similar situation from a previous case Mr Bingley had described in his accounts of the great detective, when she recalled a quote from Mr Darcy from that same journal:

The isolation of the witnesses is a most desirable arrangement, for it provides the best assurance that they have not corrupted each other's testimony. However in some cases, greater edification may arise in the discovery of a witness who is too eager to learn what the others saw, for it is likely his design is to give his own falsified account the appearance of truth by adapting it to corroborate the reports of others.

Elizabeth swallowed. Her mother had always been prying and interfering; there was no need to imagine any ulterior motives. 'Perhaps we should talk of something else. I have no wish to see you further distressed, Mamma, and debating the matter will only serve to heighten your anxiety.'

'Talk of something else? Yes, indeed, that is exactly what I have been asking for all along, is it not?' Mrs Bennet nodded at Kitty and Mary, who could only reply with bewildered expressions, for neither of them possessed the gall to contradict their agitated mother. 'Why, yes, it is indeed, only none of you would listen to me. Heaven knows I have no wish to be dwelling on such ghastly goings-on. But I do think that Mr Darcy has acted in a very high-handed and inconsiderate manner, and I shall not be sorry to see him leave our home.'

Mrs Bennet sniffed and stroked Lydia, relieved that there was one member of her ungrateful family whom she could depend upon for comfort. In truth the anxiety she exhibited was not entirely simulated. Although she had schemed to lure the detectives into her home and was confident that none could doubt she had spent the morning in her bedchamber in a state of inconsolable agitation, the suspense of awaiting the interview unsettled her. She preferred her plans to work in accordance with her own schedule, not that of Mr Darcy.

'I am sure that the inconvenience will not be long, Mamma,' said Jane, for she could not stand to see any of her family upset. 'I know you have found today very hard indeed, but perhaps you might take some comfort in knowing that these trials are not in vain. Mr Bingley gave me to understand that Mr Darcy is close to concluding his investigations.'

At this both Elizabeth and her mother turned all their attention to Jane. 'Mr Darcy believes he is close to finding the killer?' asked Elizabeth at the same time as her mother said: 'And who does Mr Darcy think is the guilty party, pray?'

Jane shook her head. 'Forgive me. I should not have spoken so. I do not know any particulars or whom Mr Darcy suspects. Indeed I do not believe that even Mr Bingley knows that. It is only that he has recognised certain behaviours and inferred from some remarks that his friend wants a little more proof to confirm his suspicions beyond any doubt. I do not think he wished me to reveal his speculations. Indeed he only mentioned it to me by way of explaining the circumstances pertaining to an entirely different matter.'

'And what matter was that, pray?' asked her mother.

Jane coloured and lowered her eyes. 'Please do not ask me to speak of it at this present time. It does not seem right to do so. I only wished to offer reassurance.'

'You said it was not to do with this singularly secretive investigation of Mr Darcy's, which he seems to consider so precious that no one is allowed to talk of it to anyone, even their own mother. If your conversation was on another matter, I see no reason why you should not speak of it to your own family. Surely Mr Darcy has not yet prohibited all conversation,' said Mrs Bennet.

'Mamma, you cannot expect Jane to discuss it if she does not wish to,' Elizabeth told her mother. 'Perhaps it was a private matter, or a subject spoken of in confidence.'

'Private matter?' Mrs Bennet's eyes lit up. 'Jane? Has Mr Bingley made you an offer? If so, there is no need for any concealment. A secret engagement might be required when the suitor has little fortune or connections to recommend himself, but with such a wealthy, handsome and amiable young gentleman as Mr Bingley there can be no doubt of your family's approval and your father's consenting to such a match.' She clapped her hands in delight at the prospect.

'Upon my word, there is no engagement,' insisted Jane. 'Please do not suppose that one exists.' She raised her fingertips to her temples and closed her eyes.

'Jane, are you feeling unwell?' asked Elizabeth.

Jane opened her eyes and gave her sister a small smile. 'It is only a headache.'

'What better time to discuss the matter? Surely, we would all take some comfort in hearing some good news to lighten our sadness.' Mrs Bennet's smile fell and she looked once more close to tears. 'I think it very cruel of you, Jane, to deny me the prospect of such joy. You have seen how much I have suffered this day and you would do nothing to lessen my grief. When I think of how much I have done for you girls! All I have ever wanted is to see my daughters happily married and you have done nothing, none of you, to help me. And now, when I am tormented by my poor nerves and most need to hear some good news, you snatch it from me!'

Jane looked exhausted and close to tears herself at this outpouring and Elizabeth squeezed her hand as she spoke to their mother: 'You cannot blame Jane for not possessing the news you wish to hear, nor expect her to mislead you simply because you feel the need for diversion. Your grief is not the only consideration to influence our actions or conversation today.'

'Lizzy.' Jane shook her head and then turned to her mother. 'Very well, Mamma, I fear the news is not as great as you wish but if it may afford you any pleasure, I shall willingly share it. Mr Bingley has asked me to write to him after the murder enquiry has ended. He insists that we should see each other again in London, when I am next in town, and that he quite depends upon returning to Hertfordshire to visit within a few months as only the prospect of returning could make leaving tolerable for him.' Jane blushed and lowered her eyes. 'He assured me of his regard and affection, but you cannot induce me to be more explicit.'

'But an understanding of that nature is nearly as good!' said Mrs Bennet. 'If a gentleman has so keen a desire to court a lady, then an offer of marriage will follow soon enough, if the lady has the sense to encourage it. To be sure, Mr Bingley is an honourable gentleman and we need not fear him going back on his word, but you must to do nothing to displease him, Jane.'

'Perhaps you might leave Jane alone, having extracted this information out of her,' suggested Elizabeth.

'No, indeed. This is a time when she needs her mother's advice the most, for she must not do anything to cause Mr Bingley to change his mind.'

'This is the price to be paid for obliging your wishes?' asked Elizabeth. 'Jane told you what you wanted to hear against her own inclinations and now you would force more instruction upon her even as we grieve for our murdered friend?'

'Lizzy, do not make a fuss,' said Jane, wincing at her sister's raised voice. For her sake, Elizabeth did not continue on the matter. Jane looked in need of peace and quiet, and there was none of that to be had in their mother's presence.

'Jane, you should get some rest. Let me help you to your room,' insisted Elizabeth.

Mrs Bennet regarded her eldest daughter. 'Oh, yes, dear Jane. In truth, you do look very drawn. Best get some rest, for it would not do for Mr Bingley to see you like this.'

Elizabeth was about to respond when Jane squeezed her arm and gave a slight shake of her head. Sisterly affection was enough to silence Elizabeth until they left the room.

'Poor Mother,' said Jane, holding her sister's arm as they walked through the hall. 'She means well, I am sure, but she certainly does provoke you, Lizzy.'

'I think you should say poor Mary and Kitty at being left alone with her. Between her exultations over your forthcoming happy news and her lamentations over the dreadful torments she alone has suffered, they shall suffer under every extreme of her disposition.'

'Lizzy, that is a little unkind to her.'

'Perhaps; although sometimes I wonder if I am unkind enough in my judgements.'

Elizabeth saw her sister's startled expression and checked herself. Jane was so kind that it grieved her to think ill of anyone, and Elizabeth did not wish to further distress her on such a dark day. She leant her head towards her sister and smiled playfully. 'You are right, Jane. I am certain our mother will occupy her thoughts with the most serious contemplations in this unhappy time. No doubt she will put a great deal of thought into which of your gowns would be most flattering dyed black for the funeral.'

14

Eager to ensure her sister's comfort, Elizabeth insisted that Jane go to bed immediately, surrounded by more than adequately puffed pillows, and then set about finding a book to read her.

'You do not have to stay here, Lizzy. Truly, it is just a headache.'

'Upon my word, no.' Elizabeth sat on the chair she had moved to Jane's bedside. 'I am determined to play the nursemaid and the companionship of Mother's nerves and impatience, delightful as they are, shall not tempt me away from you.'

Jane started to laugh but it soon became coughing.

'Jane, did you forget to take Bingley's elixir?' asked Elizabeth, concerned to hear her sister cough when she had not in days.

'Yes, I believe I did,' admitted Jane. 'I remember I was about to take my morning dose when I heard the commotion over Lydia's disappearance. I went downstairs at once and have no notion at all of where I placed the bottle. Very careless of me, I know.'

'Dear Jane, do not reproach yourself. It is no wonder you forgot such a thing with the whole house in uproar. Forgive me if I sounded accusatory; I fear I am becoming more like Mr Darcy every day.'

'Perhaps Mr Darcy has had some effect on you, but I do not think it has anything to do with the tone of your speech or the quickness of your observations,' said Jane, smiling. 'If I were to hazard my own deduction, as I know you like to call them, I should say you have quite overcome your earlier animosity towards Mr Darcy.'

'Far be it from me to contradict the first supposition of a budding detective,' said Elizabeth, her expression a more vivid confirmation of her regard than her speech. 'Least of all one not in the best of health. Perhaps I do like Mr Darcy, although he may puzzle me exceedingly at times, but at present I am far more concerned with ensuring you have your medicine.'

She stood and went over to Jane's dresser to search among the numerous small tins and bottles for the only one that did not contain one of the beauty remedies inflicted by their mother.

'Perhaps I dropped it?' suggested Jane, but after Elizabeth conducted a meticulous search under the bed and over every inch of the room, it was clear the bottle was not to be found.

'Where is it?' Elizabeth frowned. 'I wonder if the maid mistook it for one of mother's many nerve remedies and placed it in her room? I shall go and check.'

'Lizzy, please. Do not trouble yourself. I am perfectly

well enough—'

But when Jane coughed once again Elizabeth insisted. 'I shall not be long. Besides, if I cannot find your Mr Bingley's elixir, I can always fetch some of Mamma's smelling salts or laudanum or something else that should help you get some rest.'

The ante-chamber of Mrs Bennet's bedroom, which served the mistress of the house as both a dressing room and convalescence area, and thus was in frequent use, would have daunted a less determined spirit than Elizabeth's. A crammed medicine tray sat on a small table beside the winged chair in the centre of the room and a vast assortment of glassware covered the top of the dresser. If Jane's elixir had been placed in here during the confusion of the day, it would indeed be the proverbial needle in the haystack. However, such searches are by no means discouraging to the methodical detective.

Elizabeth began with the dresser and scanned the various concoctions, working from the front to back and allowing no distraction to slow her task except a brief reflection that the prosperity of their apothecary Mr Perry must owe a good deal to her mother's patronage.

After eliminating the possibility of locating Jane's elixir on the dresser, Elizabeth started towards the chair when out of the corner of her eye she noticed something amiss with the closet. The door was slightly ajar. A fleck of faint luminescence glowed from within the shadowy opening. Elizabeth approached the closet, treading on soft tiptoes. She opened the door and peered in. Pale spots and streaks gleamed weakly in the partial darkness. The source of these was no mystery: the chewed tin of luminous powder lay in the back of the closet. Numerous scratches coursed down the lowest section of the inside door. It did not require a lengthy examination to determine that they were made by a creature of Lydia's exact size.

Elizabeth bent down and touched the tin of powder. Its surface was still damp with saliva. Lydia's confinement in the closet must have been recent and however she had come to be in there, she had not been content to remain there long. The unfortunate affair of Lydia's disappearance at once seemed grotesque in its ridiculousness. The whole household had been out searching for a pug that had been trapped in the closet all along!— and at the very time that poor Harriet had been attacked and killed. It was too absurd.

Elizabeth shook her head, saddened and disgusted, but her reflections were soon intruded upon by further questions. If Lydia had been in the closet, how had she come to be found by her father and sisters in the garden? If she had somehow managed to free herself, would not Mrs Bennet have seen her? She had been resting in this very room. It was impossible that she should not have seen her pug bounding out of the closet and it seemed unlikely that Lydia should ignore the presence of her mistress and instead make her way to the garden. Indeed Elizabeth could scarcely believe that her mother would not have noticed Lydia's presence. The scratching alone would have made a clamour and surely a pug of such a raucous disposition would have barked or whined?

No, it was impossible – if her mother had been in the room. But if her mother had not been here at that time…

A crawling, sickening sensation took hold of Elizabeth's stomach. She clutched at the doorframe of the closet. She had never fainted in her life and indeed had no intention of ever doing so. However, her detective's mind had aroused a monstrous supposition and at times such as these she supposed a certain degree of nausea and head-spinning was pardonable.

She instructed herself to consider the facts. Observe and deduce. This was no time for distressing conjectures.

Elizabeth examined the closet for other clues. Most of the garments were arranged with the usual neatness, but one older walking cloak had been put away with less care than the others. She took the dark green cloak out and examined it more closely. Flecks of the luminous powder speckled its lower edges, yet she could observe no similar marks on any of the other clothes in the closet. Elizabeth looked over every inch of the cloak. There, on the front, some three inches below the left shoulder, lay a shred of tangible evidence to confirm the detective's suspicions and the daughter's fears. A strand of copper-red hair. The shade was unmistakable; too red for any of the Bennets. Surely it was Harriet's.

The cloak fell from Elizabeth's hands. Her head spun once more, but this time it was not the giddy sensation of the room swirling about her but her memories. Every instance of her mother's recent behaviour seemed to confirm her suspicions. She could not account for her mother's whereabouts at the times of any of the murders and indeed on the very morning of Charlotte's death her mother had insisted that Elizabeth accompany Mary and Kitty to Meryton on an errand. She recalled how well her father's old riding boots had matched the impressions left by the killer on the riverbank. Could not her mother have taken them from the boot cupboard and worn them just as easily as Elizabeth had done?

She had not the slightest hope of doubt. Whatever was she to do now? To act against one's own mother must surely be unthinkable, but could her conscience allow her not to act, and risk that such abominable crimes might go unanswered? She saw once more poor Charlotte's face, pale and lifeless, as she had dragged her waterlogged body from the river. In truth not one day had passed since the murder when she had not beheld her friend, not so much as a memory but an indelible vision etched in the recesses of her mind.

Elizabeth Bennet would see justice done whatever the cost, and the costs would be great. Mrs Bennet would be beyond the reach of all forgiveness and redemption. Not only herself, but all her poor family must partake in the ruination that must arise from her crimes.

How Elizabeth regretted her boasts that she would not pity the murderer nor suffer at their apprehension. She had not known herself until this moment. She had wished to be a detective, but now she wished only that she could be anything else.

Elizabeth, wishing to be anywhere but in her mother's dressing room at the moment, hurried out. She paused outside Jane's door. She had not the heart to face her sister but knew not where else to go.

'Lizzy?' Jane called. 'Is that you?'

As Elizabeth entered the room, the difference in her

countenance was so striking that Jane was at once alarmed. 'Lizzy? What is the matter?'

'I cannot tell you.'

'But what has happened? You were only gone a few minutes. What has affected such a transformation as this? Is someone hurt? Mary? Kitty?'

'No, no. No one is hurt. Pray do not alarm yourself.'

'Then whatever has distressed you so, Lizzy? I cannot be easy if you will not tell me.'

'I fear you would hate me if I told you.'

'Hate you? You know I could never do such a thing. Truly, Lizzy, you must let me know what has upset you so.'

Elizabeth bit her lip. There was such a pained expression in her sister's eyes. She glanced back at the hallway to ensure no one was present and then closed the door before approaching Jane's bed. She sat down slowly. Jane had been her confidante through every stage of her investigations. How could she refuse to tell her of this last discovery?

Elizabeth drew in a deep breath. 'Very well. I pray you will forgive me for unburdening myself of such loathsome intelligence. Oh, Jane. It is so terrible I can scarcely find the words to tell you.'

'Lizzy, please. I know you wish to put me on my guard but I believe the suspense shall only make it worse.'

'Oh, Jane. I believe our mother is one responsible for killing poor Harriet. Indeed I fear she must have murdered them all – Charlotte, Fanny, Emma – but as to Harriet I have no doubt.'

Jane whitened and shook her head. 'It cannot be. You must be mistaken. You are overcome with grief and worry. You have exhausted yourself and cannot be thinking clearly.'

'It is the truth, Jane. I wish I could believe it was a symptom of an overwrought imagination but I have discovered in her room incontrovertible evidence and every other circumstance confirms it,' Elizabeth insisted, her voice adamant, though it quavered and tears pricked her eyes.

'What proof do you have? Perhaps you have misinterpreted it in some way.'

Elizabeth told Jane of the scratch marks on the closet door and how Lydia must have been concealed inside all throughout her supposed disappearance. 'I cannot believe anyone could have been in Mamma's room without hearing the noise Lydia must have made.'

Jane considered this. 'If Lydia was in the closet, it still does not prove Mamma is a murderess, truly it does not. Perhaps she discovered Lydia but was too embarrassed at the inconvenience caused to the household to admit it, and so she let her out into the garden to be discovered by our father and sisters.'

Elizabeth shook her head. 'I cannot believe she would have concealed the pug's discovery. Mamma is not one to feel any mortification over the trouble she causes others.'

'I can more readily believe her guilty of a small untruth than committing a murder.'

'But it is not merely this on which my suspicions are based. I saw a strand of Harriet's hair upon a cloak most hastily returned to the closet. Harriet's hair was such a distinctive shade. And Mamma certainly did not wear her old walking cloak to dinner at Barton Park, nor on any other occasion that she saw Harriet.'

Jane frowned and was deep in thought for some moments. 'Well, perhaps someone else wore it? You have no proof that it was Mamma. A maid might have had opportunity to take the cloak and return it before it was missed. I cannot find it in myself to suspect anyone of our household at present, but I can more readily believe any of them a murderer than Mamma.'

'Oh, Jane. I wish I could feel persuaded. I want nothing more than to believe in our mother's innocence but I cannot at present. All I can do is hope that I am wrong.'

'But what will do you?'

'I must inform Mr Darcy of what I have discovered. I cannot conceal evidence, even if it does implicate one of our family,' said Elizabeth. 'I suppose you think I am heartless to act against my own mother's interests.'

'No, indeed. Of course you must do your duty and follow your conscience. I would never encourage you to do otherwise, especially not in a matter as serious as this.' Jane took her sister's hand in both of hers. 'If anyone can find the truth of this matter, I believe it is Mr Darcy. Mr Bingley speaks so highly of him. There may be some final clue that he can discover that will exonerate our mother and find the true culprit.'

'I wish I could think so well of everyone and believe that the happiest outcome is the most likely.' She smiled sadly at her sister. 'Dearest Jane. You look so pale, and I did not even find your elixir. A very fine nurse I would make; I go to fetch medicine and return with nothing to administer but distress.'

'Do not worry about me. I shall be fine. Go and tell Mr Darcy what you have found. Truly, Lizzy, I believe everything will work out for the best.'

15

Mrs Bennet was more than usually pleased with herself when she left the library. Her interview with Mr Darcy had gone exceedingly well; in her estimation no one could have more masterfully convinced the great detective of their innocence than she. She had enumerated the great many torments she had suffered, spoken most eloquently of how she cared for poor sweet Harriet, and furnished the gentlemen with detailed descriptions of the palpitations and nervous complaints which had troubled her since these distressing murders began. She doubted if even Mr Woodhouse could have painted a more credible picture of the symptoms of grief.

Indeed she was only sorry the interview had not been longer, for she had prepared a most moving speech on the vexations of Lydia's disappearance, but Mr Darcy wanted to know only what time she had gone up to her room and if she had seen anyone from her window. He had ended the interview in a most abrupt and high-handed fashion. She was all but dismissed from the library of her own house! Mr Darcy might very well claim to be a gentleman but there was such a want of civility in his voice, and pride in his looks, that he was nothing compared to the amiable and obliging Bingley.

Bingley pleased her greatly. She could not have imagined obtaining a better husband for her eldest daughter when she first set out to murder Charlotte Lucas. Indeed everything had gone just as she had planned, if not better. No mother could have expected a finer prize for her efforts.

Such happy reflections were brought to an abrupt close when she happened upon Elizabeth in the hallway.

'Lizzy? What are you about? You have spoken to Mr Darcy already, and I doubt there is any benefit in seeking him out again. Believe me, if I thought you had any chance there, I would encourage it, but I doubt any girl could succeed with such a conceited man, least of all you,' said Mrs Bennet.

Elizabeth looked most unsettled, her eyes fixed on the door behind her mother. 'I am here for Bingley. I believe he should see Jane. She is not well.'

'Jane? Unwell? Well, then, of course you must fetch Bingley.' Mrs Bennet nodded in earnest. 'Although she does not look so very bad, does she? Some feverish conditions can be so unbecoming.'

Elizabeth's eyes found the courage to rise to her mother's face with a pointed look. 'No. She is a little pale and her cough has returned; that is all. I wonder that you can think to inquire about such a consideration when Jane's health is at stake.'

'A careful mother must always be on the lookout for what is in her daughters' best interests. As such, you ought to fix your hair before you go in to speak to them. You look half wild. Anyone would think you had been working as a farm hand, not sitting at your sister's bedside.'

'My appearance is of no consequence.' Elizabeth moved past her mother, knocked once and then opened the library door. She had no desire to hasten her confession to Mr Darcy but conversing with her mother whilst concealing the painful emotions her presence provoked was unbearable.

Elizabeth entered the library with her mother hovering at her shoulder. Both gentlemen rose to their feet but did not attempt to hide their surprise at the interruption, though Bingley looked a vast deal happier about Elizabeth's intrusion than Darcy.

Mr Darcy's grave expression as their eyes met was nearly enough to drive away Elizabeth's nerve. It brought on a most unwelcome realisation, like a sudden and unsettling premonition, that once he knew of her mother's guilt she would never see him again. This grieved her even more than she had expected.

'Miss Bennet?' His voice broke through her thoughts and she was not sorry to cast them aside.

'Forgive me. I am sorry to intrude, but my sister Jane is not well.'

Bingley hurried across the room to Elizabeth. 'What is the nature of her complaint? It is not fever, is it? Perhaps some faintness of nerves. Such a distressing day. I should have foreseen this might have taken its toll on her delicate constitution. I blame myself for not attending to her more closely…'

'Oh no, Bingley, I cannot allow you to cast any such blame upon yourself.' Mrs Bennet swooped past Elizabeth and inserted herself between her daughter and Bingley. 'My dear Jane would feel ever so much distress if she thought she was the cause of any grief to you. I am sure her condition is not as serious as you fear, only I would wish you might take a look so as to reassure an anxious mother's nerves. Jane is quite the loveliest and sweetest of all my girls. I cannot bear to see her suffer.'

Bingley nodded. 'I shall go at once, if you would be so good as to show me the way.'

'I can go up with you to see Jane,' said Elizabeth, desperate to spare her sister from the discomfort that her mother's presence might induce. 'Mamma must be very tired, and it is no trouble for me.'

'You, go up with Bingley?' Mrs Bennet spluttered. 'No, indeed. Who better to attend to the well-being of a beloved daughter than the mother? I shall show Bingley up to see Jane, indeed I shall.' Mrs Bennet took the physician's arm and exited extolling all the virtues of her eldest daughter in a manner that only Bingley could have not found excessive.

Elizabeth looked after them with much agitation. What an unthinking sister she was! To have blurted out her suspicions to Jane and then bring about the very circumstance that should induce her mother go up to her with Bingley. She hoped Jane would forgive her for this blunder but she was by no means certain that she would forgive herself.

'Miss Bennet, perhaps I might avail myself of this opportunity to speak to you in private.' Mr Darcy's voice reminded Elizabeth of the unhappy duty before her.

She closed the door and slowly turned around to face him. There was no hostility or severity in his countenance and yet the sight of him made the task before her seem more daunting. Would he despise her once he learnt of her mother's guilt? Would she be tainted by association in his eyes? With a heart already overburdened with grief, this thought stung more than she had thought possible.

She lifted her chin and met his eyes with the unflinching courage she was determined to feign, if not entirely master. 'Indeed, Mr Darcy. I have some information I wish to tell you most urgently.'

He nodded and gestured to a winged chair by the fireplace. 'Perhaps you will have the good grace to hear me first.'

Elizabeth took the offered seat and Mr Darcy sat opposite, composing himself in a succession of attitudes: the forwards inclination of an interrogator, the upright posture of an attentive listener, and then propping one elbow on the arm of the chair and resting his jaw on his hand as though in contemplative thought. Finally, Mr Darcy elected to stand, and stationed himself by the fireplace.

'Mr Darcy, whatever it is that you wish to say to me, I believe it cannot claim more urgency than what I have to report.'

'Fear not, Miss Bennet. I shall not keep you in

suspense. The conclusion of my investigation is too near for prevarication.' Mr Darcy spoke with great rapidity as though the previous moments of silence should be compensated with haste rather than brevity of speech. 'With such powers of perception you must, I think, already possess some suspicion of the truth.'

'Indeed, you were kind enough to hint at the truth when we spoke earlier, and although I did not apprehend your meaning then, I believe I now know what you are about to tell me.'

Mr Darcy smiled. 'Of course you do. I have seldom encountered powers of observation so near equal to my own, and to find them entwined with such a singular wit and inquisitive intellect has exceeded my expectations. I am convinced that your estimable investigative talents shall only increase when your instinctive conjectures are tempered with the wisdom acquired from rigorous study and experience in the field of detection.'

'This is too much. Compliments are ill-suited to a time such as this! I beg you would excuse me from such praise and hear what I must tell you.'

'I shall not be deterred from my purpose, however much your modesty may desire it. You have heard every criticism and lecture I have levelled at you, and thus should you now receive my admiration, for it shall be expressed in no less uncompromising and forthright terms.'

'Your censure may at least have had the benefit of instruction to recommend it; praise can do nothing but flatter its recipient, and I have no wish for any at present,' Elizabeth insisted, and she looked at her hands.

'It should only serve to make what must follow more insufferable by the comparison.'

'My investigation is upon the brink of closure. If I do not seize the time now, I may never again have the opportunity. Surely a keen and perspicacious mind such as yours must already detect something of my feelings. Despite any attempts I have made to conquer or conceal my regard, you must already suspect how deeply I admire and love you.'

Elizabeth gaped. 'You love me?'

'In professing myself thus I did not expect to provoke such alarm.'

'I confess I am surprised, but it is only the prevailing circumstances that render such a declaration alarming, not its content. Indeed, in comparison with other revelations of this day, it is by no means distressing.'

'I wish I might promise never to be the means of any distress to you, but I fear that circumstances have placed such a pledge beyond my reach. Believe me now, even if you cannot do so for long, any suffering of yours shall be a greater wound to me, for I care more for your happiness than my own.'

'Please, do not commit yourself further. I fear you will regret such protestations when the truth of these murders is known.'

'Miss Bennet, I do not speak lightly,' said Mr Darcy, rather severely. Elizabeth could not help but admire that his manner could so deftly return to that of the formidable detective, and that all the softness of voice and expression which had accompanied his professions of love were abandoned with ease. 'Matters of sentiment

I generally hold to be beneath my interest but on the rare occasion when I attend to them, I do so with far greater assiduity and solemnity than the generality of men. My declaration was the result of scrupulous analysis and rigorous cogitation upon the irrevocable nature of my regard. I must insist that you do not suggest any alteration in my feelings is possible, for if it were so, I should not have spoken.'

Elizabeth took a deep breath, hoping to find comfort in claiming her usual directness. She raised her eyes to meet Mr Darcy's. 'I believe my mother is responsible, that she – that she killed Harriet.' Elizabeth's voice sounded strange to her ears, hollow, and yet it wavered less than she had anticipated. 'Indeed I believe she has been the one all along. I have no proof that she murdered Charlotte or Fanny or Emma, but I do believe she had the means and opportunity for every crime.'

Mr Darcy clapped his hands together in triumph and hurried to the chair next to her. 'Clever, loveliest Elizabeth. I should have predicted that your keen mind would ascertain the truth on your own. It would seem that I have underestimated your abilities once again.'

Elizabeth shifted so that she might face him directly. 'Then you know already of my mother's guilt?'

The corner of his mouth twitched as a courteous sympathy prevented him from laughing at such a question. 'Of course; an elementary discovery. Consider, my dear Elizabeth, that I have had the advantage of a thorough inspection of the scene of the crime and have observed numerous clues from there and on the victim's person. I came here and conducted these interviews only to corroborate what I already knew and to allow time for Sir John to summon the constables.'

'The footprints, I suppose, would have made it most clear whence the killer had come.'

'And where they returned after the crime was committed. But added to this there was a further clue in the form of a luminous substance found both on the ground and on the victim's hand.'

'That's why you looked at Lydia's face so closely. She must have gone after my mother and arrived at the scene.'

'Gone after? Not with? Why do you say that? And indeed you must relate how you came to discover your mother's guilt.'

'You wish to learn of how I solved the case?' asked Elizabeth. 'I believe I owe my understanding of the crimes to Lydia. I discovered upon the inside of my mother's closet a good deal of scratching upon the inside door.'

'Your mother's closet? So that is where she attempted to conceal the pug in order to stage its disappearance. The one particular of which I was not yet certain. How ingenious of you to make such a discovery!'

'More luck than ingenuity, I fear, but when I saw those claw marks I knew I had to examine the closet. The tin of luminous powder, the hasty manner with which my mother's cloak had been hung, upon which I found one of Harriet's hairs – all inconvertible evidence which confirmed my darkest suspicions.'

'The scrupulousness of your observations is exemplary. It must have taken great presence of mind in such a circumstance to examine the contents of the closet as soon as your attention was drawn to the matter. How few would have possessed the mental faculties or the courage to inspect the cloak! You are, my dearest Elizabeth, the finest natural detective I have ever met.'

'And the most disloyal daughter too, I should imagine. You cannot praise my capacity for detection without allowing that it signifies a proportionate want in filial duty.'

'Indeed, I do. I know too well of the predicament when honour and duty must force a detective to act in opposition to the happiness of those for whom they have the deepest affection. No one could have desired more fervently that this investigation should have led to a happier conclusion for you. I knew the likelihood of your mother's guilt some hours ago and have been in torment since. I have scrutinised every other improbable possibility in my mind, welcoming any implausible conjecture that might allow for her innocence and eliminating each only after rigorous interrogation of the facts.'

'I thank you that you took such pains on my mother's behalf and wish they had been more profitable.' She shook her head and looked away with renewed dread at what sorrow and disgrace should soon be visited on her family.

'Do not thank me on her behalf. I acted only for you.' He took her hand in his and with his other reached out to gently trace the side of her face. 'Dearest Elizabeth, I would wish for any other circumstances than these to pay my addresses. I am not a romantic man and I cannot make pretty speeches. My life has been committed to one object alone – the investigation of crime – and in you I have found a companion who shares in this vocation. I had feared that the conclusion of this case would be the end of our acquaintance, that you would despise me for exposing your mother's guilt, but you have learnt the truth for yourself and, in doing so, provided further proof of how perfectly matched we are. I must therefore ask you to consent to be my wife and fellow detective to the end of my days.'

'I hardly know how to respond to an offer made now and in such haste. We have known each other only a matter of days, and the circumstances of a murder investigation can hardly be considered propitious for forming such an attachment.'

'Inquiring minds such as ours require less than the conventional time to understand each other, and it is proof indeed of the strength of an attachment that it should arise during an investigation, when a detective has no need to seek distractions from mundane life. In any case, I am an impatient man and have no interest in courtship.'

'So it would seem, for you have attempted none,' replied Elizabeth.

'Elizabeth, there is no unfathomable mystery in my heart; it does not require a great detective to deduce my regard. My feelings cannot slow to suit convention, nor would they alter in more salubrious circumstances. Marry me or with one word silence me on the subject forever.'

'I wish I could say yes, indeed I do. I have not fully

understood my own feelings until this very day – but for me to follow them would be abominably selfish. If you will not consider your own interests, then I shall.' She took her hand back. 'It cannot be considered sensible to make such an offer after so short an acquaintance, least of all to a lady with no fortune whose entire family shall soon be hated and despised.'

'What care I for such derision? Depend upon it, when people are in need of a detective, they shall always want the best and be happy to know Mr Sherlock Darcy. My reputation and position is as secure as my fortune; I have no need of an advantageous connection in marriage.'

Elizabeth smiled in spite of herself. 'Well, I am pleased at least to see that neither your proposal nor my refusal have induced any affectation of humility. Modesty would suit you ill – or at least I suppose it would, if I should ever see it.'

'Indeed, there is nothing becoming or honourable in conduct that is neither justified nor true to one's character. I have never known your actions to be determined by anything other than your own will. If you do not wish to marry me, say so and I will never speak of it again. Do not declare that you would like to, but will not or cannot.'

'I would accept if my own feelings were my only consideration, but they are not,' said Elizabeth firmly, although it pained her to be the cause of the wounded expression in his eyes. 'You dismiss my objections out of hand because it suits your motive to do so, not because they do not require deliberation.'

He replied in an instant with a triumphant look. 'On the contrary, I am more than willing to deliberate any objections you raise. Enumerate as many objections as you wish; I shall conquer them all!'

Elizabeth shook her head. 'No, please; I have no wish to argue, least of all at present. Can we not agree to defer all discussion of future plans until the murder investigation has been resolved?'

He paused, stood and returned to his stance by the fireplace. 'As you wish. At least in the investigation we shall agree, as it seems we are both well aware of the facts of the case. The constables will arrive presently. There is the physical evidence of Miss Smith's hair on the cloak and the phosphorescent powder; and that will be the end of it, for today at least.'

'Yet I fear that even with the addition of the footprint at the scene of the crime, this will not amount to an unassailable case against my mother. And what of the other murders? There is no material evidence to link her to those.'

'That is unfortunate, but you must consider that your mother is the only person amongst all of your family and the servants of Longbourn who was not seen and accounted for during the time of the crime. Surely you do not doubt her guilt?'

'No. Yet I believe that my family would seize upon any implausible alternative if it were offered.'

'Then I propose a stratagem whereby we distract her with some other matter that should preoccupy her thoughts and provoke an unguarded emotional response, then press her for a confession.'

After a moment's consideration, Elizabeth's eyes brightened and she gave him a playful grin. 'As regards the previous matter of our conversation, I should inform you, Mr Darcy, that I have quite changed my mind. I shall marry you – and I think we should announce it as soon as may be.'

16

Mrs Bennet, vexed at the prospect of Bingley seeing Jane in a state of unprepossessing health, commanded the servants to search the house for the misplaced elixir. It was soon discovered on a sideboard on the ground floor and, under Bingley's tender ministrations, Jane was relieved of her cough in time to return to the drawing room with the rest of the family to hear Mr Sherlock Darcy's announcement. Mr Bennet and Mr Darcy were the last to join the gathering, owing to a second private discourse between them in the library.

Lydia raised her head from her mistress' lap as the illustrious detective swept into the room but as he did not repeat any of his previous attentions to her, she resolved to ignore him and settled back down to nuzzle Mrs Bennet's hand.

Mr Darcy took command of the room from a position by the fireplace, standing before Bingley and the Bennets, gratified by the arrangement of the surroundings.

Many guests preferred the drawing room above any other in Longbourn as it possessed large windows looking out into the gardens and therefore was less gloomy than most of the house. Indeed the abundance of light was such that Mrs Bennet's floral furnishings and her pink flocked wallpaper appeared a little less ridiculous than the décor in the darker rooms. However, the primary reason for Mr Darcy's choice of this room was the configuration of furniture which allowed the Bennet family to be seated in an arc around him, but facing one another.

It was Darcy's custom whenever he wished to make dramatic revelations concerning the results of his investigations to gather the suspects together and stand before them to recount the key points of the case. He saw no reason why the same practice should not also be applied when announcing an engagement to be married.

'No doubt some of you are wondering why I have asked you all here,' he began. 'It is because I have something of the most utmost importance to announce. Some of you may find it shocking but I assure you all, what I am about to tell you is the incontrovertible truth.'

Mr Sherlock Darcy's speech was building an elegant rhythm, but he paused to observe the nervous glances being exchanged between Bennets.

'I have spoken already to Mr Bennet and he has reluctantly come to understand the veracity of my conclusions, and concurs that I have most scrupulously adhered to my methods of sound, unbiased observation and logical deduction.'

Mr Bennet, realising that his wife and daughters'

pointed gazes were now fixed upon him, shifted in his scrolled-wing chair and cleared his throat. 'Ahem. Yes, that is to say, correct. Quite so. Mr Darcy has indeed assured me of the strength of his convictions in the most vigorous terms.'

Elizabeth gave her father a sympathetic smile. He looked more perplexed than amused. She suspected he had found his brief interview with Mr Darcy rather a trying experience. It was most unfair that tradition dictated that the man of the house had to be consulted on all matters concerning their family. She felt it would have been kinder to leave her father in peace and then, once the matter had been settled, break the news to him over a glass of port.

'My good friend Bingley and I first arrived in the neighbourhood with a single purpose – to investigate the mysterious deaths of three young ladies,' Mr Darcy continued, pacing back and forth on the pink rug and lending more gravitas to the décor than it deserved. 'Since my inquiries began another victim, Miss Harriet Smith, has fallen prey to a most brutal and savage attack. I have been convinced since the outset of my investigations that these deaths were no mere confluence of accidents and unconnected attacks, but the work of one most rapacious and determined killer.'

The Bennets gasped, though they were hardly shocked by this revelation, as Elizabeth had said the same to them on numerous occasions. However, the abrupt pause following Mr Darcy's impressive speech demanded some response. It would have been ungracious not to gasp.

Mr Darcy regarded his audience with a hawkish

expression. 'I have seldom found any pleasure in residing in the country and, with a case as serious as this, I naturally was impatient to discover the identity of the killer as soon as possible.'

'Indeed, I can attest to that,' said Bingley. 'While Darcy conducts every investigation with indefatigable vigour, I have seldom seen him set about a case with greater urgency or haste.'

'Your tendency to embellish your descriptions of my investigative methods notwithstanding, you have most correctly articulated my approach in this instance, Bingley, when you call it "haste". Indeed it was this haste that led me to make a most unfortunate and regrettable mistake: I underestimated the clever and resourceful mind of Miss Elizabeth Bennet.'

This time the family's gasps owed nothing to the skill of Mr Darcy's oratory.

Elizabeth threw up her hands. 'I do not understand why you are all looking at me like that. "Clever" and "resourceful" are not synonyms for guilty. Why should you assume that Mr Darcy would praise my abilities only in order to accuse me of murder?'

'Of course, no one could possibly think you are guilty of hurting anyone, Lizzy.' Jane patted her sister on the arm.

'Indeed, Miss Bennet, you are correct. Your sister has been guilty of nothing but assisting my investigations.'

'As you all know, I am fond of sketching and it has been my habit to take my pencils and paper on my morning walks,' Elizabeth explained to her mystified family. 'When I was left alone with poor Charlotte on the day we found her in the river, I decided to draw the scene to the best of my ability. This drawing has proved of some use to Mr Darcy, as have some of my other investigations into the murders.'

'Lizzy! You do not mean to tell me that you have been scampering about the countryside drawing corpses!' Mrs Bennet shrieked. 'Have you no feminine delicacy? I must say that I think it most disagreeable. Mr Bennet, kindly tell your daughter she must destroy these loathsome sketches and in future restrict her artistic urges to flowers and landscapes.'

'Technically, a crime scene is a landscape,' Elizabeth informed her.

Mrs Bennet glared at her daughter before redirecting her outrage at her husband. 'Mr Bennet!'

'It is of very little matter to me what Lizzy chooses to draw,' replied her husband. 'If she is sketching corpses then at least she is not troubling anyone living to sit still for hours to have their portrait taken. I find it very tiresome when a lady's accomplishments can only be exhibited at the expense of a good deal of time and inconvenience to others.'

Mrs Bennet let out a frustrated sigh and her sentiments were echoed by a low growl from Lydia.

Mr Bennet gave her a cheerful grin. 'Come now, my dear, if Mr Darcy does not object to her drawing, why should we?'

'Well said, Mr Bennet. Indeed I am very far from objecting to your daughter practising her considerable talent in this area,' said Mr Darcy. 'I am convinced that with more experience she shall rise to pre-eminence as

England's foremost crime portraitist.'

'You do not mean to encourage my daughter in this odious pursuit, and worse to do so openly, so that everyone should know?' Mrs Bennet spluttered. A weaker woman would have required smelling salts. 'I will not allow it. In any case, I am sure she will have little occasion to gain more experience, as you call it, for I am determined that she shall not venture out of doors again. Not after poor sweet little Harriet was attacked so close to Longbourn.'

'I believe I can promise you that Hertfordshire shall soon be safe from these savage attacks,' said Mr Darcy. 'In any case such prohibitions may prove immaterial. I have made your daughter an offer of marriage. Even if you were to forbid Miss Elizabeth Bennet to pursue such endeavours, Mrs Sherlock Darcy shall always be thrown into the path of sinister mysteries.'

The transformation of Mrs Bennet's countenance was indeed something to behold; from seething outrage to astonishment to giddy happiness in a blink of an eye. 'You? Marry Elizabeth?' she stammered. 'Oh, is this not wonderful! Indeed this is most gratifying to hear, Mr Darcy. You know from the very day you stepped into our home I felt sure something would come of it, indeed I did – a mother senses these things you know – I knew you and my Lizzy would fall in love. Did I not say so, girls, in this very room?' She appealed to her daughters but they looked awkwardly away.

'Mamma, please,' said Elizabeth, frowning at her mother. 'You forget that you have not heard my answer.'

'You cannot possibly have refused,' she scoffed. 'My

Lizzy is no simpleton. You cannot expect that it is likely another offer would ever be made to you, certainly not one from a gentleman the equal of Mr Darcy. And I am sure he must be the one gentleman in England that might tolerate this morbid fancy of yours to draw dead people.'

'Indeed I believe he may be, Mamma. But I do not mean to confine my abilities to simply drawing. I am also greatly interested in detection and it is my intention to study all areas of criminology. I would not be happy to be simply a wife, even a wife whose husband, as you put it, *tolerates* her practicing the art of crime portraiture. I am going to become a detective.'

'Indeed, she has an excellent aptitude for observation and logical deduction,' Mr Darcy declared. 'Once she has improved her understanding of criminal theory, analytical chemistry, anatomy, and the geography of London's underworld through extensive reading, she will prove a most capable detective. She has consented to study and work as an apprentice with me in London.'

'Apprentice? I am convinced you said I should be your partner when you spoke of this earlier, Mr Darcy. It is a most inauspicious beginning to my career if I am to be demoted in under an hour,' remarked Elizabeth.

'Partner? No, indeed I did not; but we could say you are to be my protégée, if you prefer.'

'I suppose that will have to do. For now at least.'

'Lizzy! I do not care what title you prefer, I will not allow it unless you tell me you will marry Mr Darcy,' insisted a seething Mrs Bennet. 'Live in London unmarried and take up a profession, scampering about drawing gruesome bodies and playing detective? Fie! You would be ruined, and your poor sisters too. No, I will not have it! I would see you dead first.'

A heavy silence fell upon the room. The violence in Mrs Bennet's voice and the malice in her eyes were felt by all; even Lydia slunk off her mistress' lap and sought refuge on Jane in case Mrs Bennet was angry with her or, worse yet, going to shut her in a closet again.

Elizabeth, though she had known of her mother's guilt, felt that this was the first moment she had seen the force behind it. Was that expression of hateful rage the last thing that Charlotte and the others ever beheld? The very thought sent a shiver through her, but she steeled her nerve and looked at her mother with unflinching determination. 'Alas, I can believe that all too well, Mamma. But you need not trouble yourself in this instance. I have already agreed to marry Mr Darcy.'

'Indeed, I have spoken to Mr Bennet already and Elizabeth and I are to be married. It is all quite settled.' Mr Darcy waved his hand dismissively.

'I say, that is splendid news. Well, my warmest congratulations to you both,' said Bingley, eager to have the atmosphere lightened. He rose to his feet to shake his friend's hand and added in a hushed voice: 'I must say, Darcy, you are a dark horse. I had no idea! You quite beat me to it, Darcy, although perhaps not for long…' He glanced back at Jane and then returned to his seat.

'Well, that is excellent news,' interrupted Mrs Bennet, not having heard Bingley speak as she desperately sought to resume the countenance of a proud and joyous mother. 'How pleased I am for you both. The happy event cannot be too soon for me, although you must give me time to make all the arrangements…'

'I suggest that you desist from making any plans for our wedding in the foreseeable future,' said Mr Darcy. 'You forget that I declared I would not consider returning to London until I had found the killer.'

'So you intend to say some while longer, then?' Mrs Bennet inquired. 'That is good. London weddings are all very well, but I should much rather that Lizzy was married from Longbourn where the whole neighbourhood might see.'

'Regretfully, we shall not be able to oblige your preferences as concerns the nuptials,' said Mr Darcy. 'The mystery is at an end. I know who is responsible for the attack on Miss Harriet Smith and three other unfortunate victims.'

A chilled silence fell upon the room and Lydia, who was never one to miss an opportunity to seek attention, let out an excited yip and returned to her mistress' lap to lick her hand. Mrs Bennet did not acquiesce to her pug's bid for affection as she was a good deal too busy contemplating whether peonies or roses would look better in the church and whether she would have time send away to London for the best lace. She had only half a mind left to listen to Mr Darcy rattling on about his investigation and she would not have even given him that courtesy were he not soon to become her son-in-law. It was of no matter to her whom the great detective imagined responsible for the deaths. She knew she had outwitted him; his engagement to Lizzy confirmed what Mrs Bennet had believed all along – she was above suspicion. What did it matter if she had lost her temper earlier? She doubted anyone had noticed and even if they had, it did not signify anything except that she was a most particular and careful mother.

'Well then, Darcy, do not keep us in suspense,' urged Bingley. 'If you have unravelled this mystery and discovered the identity of the fiend who attacked the young ladies, let us hear how you deduced it.'

Mr Darcy rapped his fingers on the mantel before taking a step forward from the fireplace to address them. 'It was apparent from the first that it was unlikely three young ladies would be attacked by different assailants, but improbable as that was I could not eliminate the possibility of multiple murderers without physical evidence. Fortunately I was in possession of an excellent portrait of the scene of Miss Lucas' drowning, showing the tracks and footprints in the riverbank, and thus I ascertained the particulars and characteristics of the killer's movements. There is no doubt in my mind that these tracks were identical to those at the spot where Miss Harriet Smith was savagely attacked this morning – tracks that led straight back to this very house!'

His audience started at this dramatic revelation, but Mrs Bennet paid him no such attention. 'Did they indeed?' she declared with a derisive snort. 'Well, I do not claim to understand any of this nonsense about footprints and so forth, Mr Darcy, indeed I do not. I cannot see how anyone's steps should look any different from another person's, and it seems to me that peering in the dirt is a most ungentlemanly way to go about things.'

'I assure you that many juries have been convinced

by the evidence of footprints, Mrs Bennet, even if you are not. Besides which, I did not say it was footprints that connected Longbourn to the scene of the crime, but *tracks*. Tracks of a far more distinctive nature.' He strode back towards the fireplace.

'Forgive me, Darcy, I do not follow. If there were no footprints, then how can you have identified the murderer from the tracks? If the tracks were those of a horse or carriage, then the killer might have been anyone,' said Bingley.

'The only logical inference is that the tracks were made by the feet of the killer,' explained Elizabeth, 'but that the tracks were not those of a person.'

'Precisely.' Mr Darcy turned to face his audience, raising his arm as though he were wielding an invisible sword. 'The tracks were indeed those of a canine, a small breed of dog. That much would be apparent to even the untrained eye, but to Sherlock Darcy, who has studied the tracks of every breed of domestic animal, they were undoubtedly the tracks of a female pug dog. A pug dainty of foot but round of girth, given the weight required to make the depth of impression. They were the same distinctive tracks I beheld on the first day I came to Longbourn, when a dog of that kind scampered around the hedges and pawed at the soft earth. They were incontrovertibly the prints of that pug dog sitting there upon you, Mrs Bennet!'

It must be observed that of all the shocked expressions in the room, there was not a face amongst them that conveyed more astonishment than that of Mrs Bennet.

'This is outrageous! How could you accuse my poor

sweet Lydia? Indeed, I never heard such nonsense in all my life!' Mrs Bennet declared in a most affronted tone and Lydia, although oblivious to the allegations against her character, echoed her mistress' sentiments with a loud yip.

'I must say, Mr Darcy, that if this is some kind of joke, it is a most tasteless one,' Mr Bennet agreed. 'A gentleman cannot go about calling upon a man to ask for his daughter's hand in marriage one minute and then accuse his wife's pug of murder the next. No, it will not do. It is most irregular behaviour indeed.'

'I make no apologies for what you perceive as an apparent irregularity in my conduct, sir. I have spoken the truth. Can any among you account for the dog's whereabouts at the time of Miss Smith's death?'

Mrs Bennet fumed. 'Of course we cannot. Everyone knows my poor Lydia was missing this morning, but she is perfectly innocent. Why, my Lydia would not harm a fly! To imagine that my dear, sweet little pug could possibly hurt any of those girls is the most hateful, despicable nonsense I have ever heard in my life! Even if she wished to, how could such a small dog be any threat to fully grown ladies?'

'In the usual circumstances, a pug is no threat to anyone, but even the smallest dog, if possessed of a crafty and malevolent spirit, may form a deadly intent upon on its prey. In the case of Miss Lucas, the pug chased her down the riverbank and caused her to fall. With the same savage energy did the dog spring upon Miss Price in the churchyard, and in the pale light of dawn, with the vicious gleam of murderous intent in the creature's eyes, it may well have seemed to the girl that it was a beast of hell that charged and sent her down to dash her head against the tombstone.'

'Murderous intent? Beast of hell? I never heard such vile, ridiculous slander. No one could believe anything of the kind about my darling Lydia, no matter what you have to say, Mr Darcy,' declared Mrs Bennet.

'I assure you, Sir John will believe me,' replied Mr Darcy. 'I have evidence enough to persuade him that the dog must be put to death for the safety of all. The first two deaths merely whetted the pug's appetite for murder and she set upon her next prey, Miss Emma Woodhouse. In a vicious frenzy, the dog charged at the horse as the lady was riding, causing the beast to rear up and Miss Woodhouse to fall to her death. Her attack on Miss Smith was one of a most savage brutality. The victim was first knocked to the ground, then the dog seized her in its jaws and tore out her throat.'

Elizabeth looked as the collective shudder and horrified gasps rippled through the father and sisters, and felt most acutely for how the description had unsettled them. Only her mother was unaffected by Mr Darcy's invention.

'You are lying! Lydia did not bite Harriet at all. If there was any tearing to the girl's throat, it must have been done after she was strangled.'

Mr Darcy turned to face Mrs Bennet with an expression that even Elizabeth, with all her feelings of devotion and admiration for the detective, had to concede was very smug indeed.

'Indeed you are correct, Mrs Bennet. There was not a

single bite mark on Miss Smith. She was, as you correctly say, strangled, a fact you could know only if you were the one who killed her!'

'Oh no! Perhaps there has been some misunderstanding?' suggested Jane.

'Oh hush, you silly girl,' Mrs Bennet snapped. 'It is most clear that Mr Darcy has set upon destroying this family, and your father intends to challenge him to a duel for impugning my honour and Lydia's.'

'Intend to what?' Mr Bennet spluttered.

'There will be no duels, Mrs Bennet,' Mr Darcy declared. 'This is a matter of justice and your crimes will be dealt with by the proper authorities.'

Mr Bennet made a valiant attempt to conceal his relief. 'Yes, that would be the only proper and gentlemanly way to deal with such a grave matter as murder, had any such crime been committed, but I still cannot believe that my wife is guilty of these crimes.'

'Indeed. I should much rather thoroughly consider the case for some misunderstanding, just as Miss Bennet suggested,' agreed Mr Bingley.

'But she knew how Harriet was killed,' Elizabeth reminded him. 'Surely you can see no innocent explanation for that.'

'There is yet one further vital piece of evidence against Mrs Bennet,' said Mr Darcy. 'When I recently examined the body of the late Miss Harriet Smith, I detected a faintly luminous substance upon the back of her right hand. It was the distinctive glow of a phosphorescent powder, traces of which still remain on the pug's face as we speak. The very same cosmetic powder that Mrs

Bennet purchased from one Mr Perry!'

'That proves nothing,' insisted Mrs Bennet. 'It is true that I may have purchased such a product but I believe it to have been stolen some two days ago. Quite well before the time when Miss Smith was attacked.'

'That is not true, Mamma,' said Elizabeth. 'The powder was in your closet. The very place you concealed Lydia this morning to provide you with the opportunity leave the house unnoticed.'

'You mean to say you had us off searching the gardens all morning and the confounded animal was in your closet all along?' Mr Bennet looked most aggrieved.

'Indeed she did.' Elizabeth took out the chewed tin of powder from its place of concealment under the cushion beside her. 'Mamma, please do not perjure yourself any further. I have seen the scratches Lydia made on your closet door. Mr Darcy is right. He has incontrovertible evidence against you. You cannot deny what you have done.'

'Fie, you ungrateful girl. Turn on your own mother, would you? Accuse me of lying in my own house?' Mrs Bennet spluttered. 'How could you, you unfeeling creature? When I think of all that I have done for you!'

'All that you have done for me?'

'Indeed! Everything I have ever done has been for you and your sisters. For years I have worked to improve your prospects, though I had little charm or beauty with which to work. How dare you look at me with such ingratitude! Mr Darcy would have never noticed a plain thing like you if you had not been part of his investigation,' she sneered. 'I killed those girls and I would gladly do so again if it would do half as much to help my daughters! You cannot deny that you and Jane have already benefited from my actions. Why, Darcy and Bingley would never have stepped into the neighbourhood if it were not for me. You will forever be in my debt.'

'No, I will not. I have nothing but contempt and hatred for what you have done, and I refuse to let you blame me and my sisters for this evil. I would have done everything in my power to prevent you had I known. I would have given my own life if it could have saved our friends.'

'Give your own life? Such noble words, Lizzy. Do you think you have the courage to act on them?' Mrs Bennet sprang from the couch, launching Lydia onto the floor. She grabbed Elizabeth, pulling her to her feet and twisting her arm behind her back. The chewed tin of phosphorescent powder she had been holding clattered to the ground and was immediately set upon by the pug. Before Darcy or Bingley was halfway across the room Mrs Bennet grabbed a silver letter-opener from the writing table and held it at her daughter's throat.

'Perhaps there is a way for you to repay my kindness after all, Lizzy. Mr Darcy, you will open the doors to the garden over there, if you please. We would not want any harm to come to your betrothed, would we?'

'She is lying,' Elizabeth insisted, despite her mother pressing the letter-opener more firmly against her throat. 'She will not hurt me.'

Lydia growled and snorted as she licked the remnants of delicious powder from the tin at Elizabeth's feet, acting, somewhat unintentionally, as sentry guard for Mrs Bennet's hostage.

'I fear you might have misjudged your mother, my dearest Elizabeth. I believe she is more than capable of hurting you a great deal indeed.' Mr Darcy replied, his expression one of acute concern. He hurried across the room and opened the doors to the back garden.

Mrs Bennet edged her way to the door, forcing her daughter in front of her. 'I will take the carriage and Elizabeth and Lydia will come with me. You are not to inform anyone that I have left, or Lizzy will not make it back. If no one follows us, then I will release Elizabeth in a few hours and she will have to make her way back home by post. Is that understood?'

The Bennets, Bingley and Darcy nodded mutely. Lydia, who had coated much of her face with a slobbery sheen of luminous saliva, trotted over to her mistress with the tin still in her jaws and growled as if in accordance with the arrangement.

'Mamma, you cannot really go through with this despicable plan,' Jane urged. 'Lizzy is your daughter.'

'Would you see your mother hang?' Mrs Bennet glared back. 'Would you have me condemned for doing what was necessary to help you wretched girls find husbands?'

'I think our gratitude would be more forthcoming,' Elizabeth muttered through her imperilled throat, 'if you had not paved the path to our husbands with the murdered corpses of our friends.'

'Dearest Elizabeth, I do not think that this is the most opportune time to raise your objections to your mother's methods.' Mr Darcy held the door to the garden open as Mrs Bennet jostled Elizabeth towards the exit.

'Mr Darcy, if you would be so good as to stand back a little distance from the door,' Mrs Bennet instructed. 'I am not such a fool as to risk you impeding my escape.'

Mr Darcy stepped back. 'Of course not. I would only ask for the opportunity to say farewell to your daughter.'

'I am surprised, Mr Darcy. I had not thought you at all sentimental.'

'In situations such as these, Mrs Bennet, I believe even the most reserved and taciturn of gentlemen would seek to make his wishes known to the lady he loves.'

Mrs Bennet steered Elizabeth in front of her to face Mr Darcy. 'There you are, Lizzy. I am not as callous as you would think. Hold out your hand to Mr Darcy so he might have his kiss goodbye.'

'I think it very ill that you should instruct me on how to conduct my farewells when you have a blade poised at my throat,' said Elizabeth.

'Fie, girl, why would you argue with me when I try to show you and your Mr Darcy some kindness? Such ungrateful disobedience.' In her agitation Mrs Bennet felt the letter-opener twitch in her hand, as though urging itself to press deeper into the neck. Elizabeth flinched. 'Hold out your hand to Mr Darcy or you shan't ever see him again.'

Elizabeth released what was, in her mother's opinion, a most disagreeably petulant sigh and held out her hand.

Mr Darcy bent forward, took her hand and kissed it. 'Be careful. I hope you will endeavour to treat your mother with as much civility as I was obliged to show the kidnapper in the case of the vanishing governess.'

'Indeed, Lizzy. You would do well to treat your mother with a little more—' Mrs Bennet was interrupted by her daughter's heel delivering a swift and rather brutal kick to her shin.

The momentary distraction was all Mr Darcy needed. He darted forward, seizing Mrs Bennet's wrist. The letter opener fell to the floor. Lydia, beside herself with excited fury, jumped and nipped at Mr Darcy until Elizabeth grabbed her by the scuff of her furry neck and pulled her away. The offended pug yelped and expressed her displeasure by biting Mr Bingley, who had hurried over to join in the fray, before scampering through the door into the garden.

Mrs Bennet struggled and screamed every sort of abuse and insult at Mr Darcy even as he ushered her to the open door, where Sir John and his two constables had appeared from their concealed locations in the garden.

'Mrs Bennet? Well I never,' said Sir John, his bristling eyebrows conveying even more astonishment than his words. 'I should have never have believed it possible.'

'Sir John, you must assist me,' insisted Mrs Bennet. 'This man has most falsely and unjustly accused me in my own home, and now he would manhandle me as though I were some ruffian. Surely you cannot allow such shameful slander and vile abuse of an innocent lady!'

'Now, now, Mrs Bennet.' Sir John puffed out his chest and raised his finger with all the grave authority of a magistrate. 'We heard your confession and your threats against your own daughter. You have been most unfortunate in your choice of witnesses.'

'Mr Bennet! Will you not speak for me?' Mrs Bennet cried out to her husband, realising she had no hope of appealing to Sir John or of breaking free on her own. 'How can you sit there while your wife is so grossly mistreated?'

'No, Mrs Bennet, I will not.' Mr Bennet rubbed his forehead and stood up to address his wife. 'For many years I have tolerated your nagging and berating of our daughters, for I saw no danger in it and sought only to get some measure of peace. But that you killed those poor young girls, that you would threaten my Lizzy, and have the gall to say it was for them that you so acted. No, Mrs Bennet. Such crimes as these are not to be forgiven, and I am heartily ashamed of myself for failing to perceive or prevent such wickedness.'

The rest of the Bennets looked helplessly at one another. There was nothing at all to be done. Mr Darcy delivered Mrs Bennet into the custody of Foster and Granley.

'Capital work, Mr Darcy,' declared Sir John. 'I am pleased to see this ghastly business cleared up. Never let it be said of this magistrate that he spared any expense for the safety and well-being of his neighbours. If ever a mystery in my jurisdiction requires a detective, then I shall not settle for anything but the best.'

'Indeed, Sir John.' Mr Darcy bowed his head with curt politeness but Elizabeth detected a tightness in his lips as he did so. She suspected him of having no higher opinion of the pompous Sir John than she had herself. 'I doubt you will have any trouble with this case. It has reached a most irrefutable conclusion.'

'Quite so.' Sir John nodded, and motioned to his constables that it was time to escort their prisoner from the premises.

'I expect this is goodbye for us all, Mamma,' said Elizabeth.

'Goodbye, my daughters and husband. I hope in time you will understand that whatever I have done, I sought only to ensure the happiness of my dear family,' said Mrs Bennet, in the most affectionate tone she could muster, before her eyes fell on the detective who had ensnared her. There was no trace of sweetness in her voice when she addressed him. 'And Mr Darcy. Goodbye to you, too.'

The constables departed with Mrs Bennet. Sir John, thinking it best to remain with the family, joined them as a bewildered Mr Bennet closed the doors on the garden.

'Well, this has been a most unexpected turn of events, make no mistake,' he declared. His lips twitched as he considered the proper course of action, for this was a sensitive situation and required the utmost tact and delicacy. 'No doubt it has come as rather a shock to you all. A most unpleasant business but you need not fear any reproach from me. You are all quite above suspicion in this case and I would not have you, my dear Bennets, tormenting yourself with thoughts of how your wife and mother came to commit these dreadful crimes without your knowledge. It does not do to dwell too much over these things, you understand. I had a pointer once that quite wasted away from grief. Simply would not eat. I dare say you might all feel better with a spot of tea and I wager the restorative property of a little food should you do a world of good.' He patted his ample stomach, pleased that with this advice he had been able to prove himself a most sympathetic and attentive neighbour to this unfortunate family in their hour of need.

'Indeed,' murmured Mr Bennet, but he looked so distracted that it was quite left to Jane to make the necessary arrangements.

Once Sir John was certain he had given the Bennets the full benefit of his recommendations for their teatime refreshments and dining arrangements, and assured them he would send them a joint of pork and a pheasant or two, he joined Elizabeth and Darcy by the window observing the departure of Mrs Bennet. 'You have done a splendid job here, Darcy, no two ways about it.'

'Indeed he has, Sir John,' replied Elizabeth. 'I confess I doubted whether a confession should be procured from my mother but now I am persuaded no person exists who might elude Mr Darcy. I am sure he could provoke anyone into careless speech.'

Sir John was less capable of following Elizabeth's arch tone than was her fiancé, who turned to face her and exchange a knowing smile. Indeed the magistrate felt some awkwardness in addressing the daughter of a murderess on matters other than condolences or culinary guidance. 'Oh. Yes. Quite so, quite so.'

His murmur was echoed faintly by the sound of barking in the garden and three pairs of eyes observed that

Mrs Bennet had broken free from the constables and was fleeing towards the shrubbery.

'I do hope they are able to catch her without too much trouble,' said Elizabeth. 'I fear they should have used restraints.'

'Fear not, Miss Eliza. She has no chance of escape.' Sir John puffed out his chest. 'Foster has outpaced many a poacher. There was one wiry scamp it took him a full hour to run down, but run him down he did.'

'Indeed, her pace has slackened already and Foster fast gains on her – but I believe Granger shall be the one to recapture her,' said Mr Darcy.

'I cannot agree with you there, Darcy. Foster nearly has her,' said Sir John, but his pride transformed into astonishment. 'Well, I say! I never saw such a thing. She has only gone and dealt poor Foster a most vicious blow in the gut.'

'Yes, but Granger will soon have her, although that dog of your mother's is proving something of a nuisance,' Mr Darcy observed to Elizabeth.

They watched as Granger lunged at the fugitive whilst Foster contended with the excited pug darting around them and nipping at their heels.

'Well, would you look at that! Granger has gone and caught her after all.' Sir James shook his head and chuckled. 'I should never wager against you knowing what's what, Mr Darcy. It's beyond me how you predict such a turn of events.'

'An elementary calculation based on observation of the facts, Sir John.'

'If I might venture my own supposition, I should say

that Granger did not anticipate that my mother would elbow him so viciously,' said Elizabeth. She winced in sympathy as the winded constable doubled over again, while the other was tripped by a pug-shaped missile.

'Indeed, he did not,' agreed Mr Darcy. 'However, I am certain they have now apprehended the full threat their fugitive presents. They will not leave her arms free when they secure her.'

'No, indeed they will not,' said Sir John stoutly. 'Still, one can hardly reproach them for going easy on her at first. It is most astonishing. They cannot have expected that a lady would possess such vigour or be capable of such violence.'

Elizabeth considered it an act of prodigious forbearance that she did not observe to Sir John it was under his instruction that the constables had not restrained her mother, and that not expecting a murderess to be capable of violence seemed most foolish indeed. She imagined that Jane would have been quite proud of her if she had been able to hear the conversation.

Sir John glimpsed something of Elizabeth's wry expression, and misinterpreted it. 'Oh! You must excuse my unguarded speech, Miss Elizabeth. I should not have spoken of your mother so frankly before you. If you thought I meant any slight on your family, I am mortified, my dear girl. I assure that that I consider the Bennets with the utmost respect and…'

'Please, sir, do not make yourself uneasy on my account. There was no offence in your speech. You have always been most kind to my family and I expect such friends shall soon be in short supply. Your observations about my mother were just and accurate, and certainly no more severe than my own.'

'Ah, yes, well. Very good.' Sir John coughed, nodded his head, and gestured at the window, where the two constables had at last successfully closed upon their escapee. 'A-ha! Look at that. They have her now. Capital, capital.'

'Indeed they do.' Elizabeth sighed. 'I suppose that is the end of this business, for today at least.' Her hand brushed against Mr Darcy's and they interlocked fingers as they watched the constables frogmarch Mrs Bennet into the distance.

The three observers at the window said nothing as Mrs Bennet was led out of view. Very soon there was nothing left in the garden except a small beige pug staring off after her mistress with her left front paw raised in solemn adieu. It is a testament to the deep and loyal affection felt by Lydia that she stood thus for a full twenty seconds before catching the scent of some enticing creature in a nearby hedge that was simply begging to be chased.

Sir James was the first to turn away from the window. 'I hear I am to congratulate you both on your forthcoming betrothals.'

Darcy and Elizabeth informed him that this was indeed so, and acknowledged his good wishes with due courtesy.

'I must say that it was very decent of you, Miss Eliza, not to hold any of this business against Darcy. It shows uncommonly good sense and liberality. There's many a lady who might have refused the gentleman and blamed him once he informed her of her mother's guilt.'

'Indeed, there may well be, Sir James,' said Darcy, 'but in this case, it was not incumbent on me to inform Miss Bennet of anything that she had not already deduced for herself.'

Sir James's astonishment could not be concealed. 'You mean to say she knew about all this already?'

'I only learnt of my mother's guilt this afternoon,' Elizabeth explained. 'I assure you I have not acted as an accessory to her crimes.'

'Indeed, she informed me of her suspicions immediately. Her conduct in this investigation has been above reproach,' said Darcy. He looked so proud and happy to say as much that Elizabeth did not remind him that he had previously found a good deal to reproach in her investigative endeavours.

'Yes, yes, I am sure that is so, but how did she come to apprehend any of it before you told her? You cannot mean to tell me that the dear girl found out on her own.'

'Indeed, Sir James, let me assure you that I most certainly did,' replied Elizabeth.

'Surely not?' Sir James looked at Darcy who only nodded in assent. 'But how did she happen to stumble upon the truth of the matter when it has eluded everyone else for so long?'

'Stumble? I suppose you have witnessed my dancing, but I believe I make a comparatively surefooted detective,' said Elizabeth with a laugh. 'As to how I came to realise the truth, I would say that it was the curious incident of the pug in the closet that first aroused my suspicions.'

'A pug in a closet?' Sir John blinked in astonishment.

'Well, I cannot see how that signifies anything, my dear girl, but I suppose we must put it down to a woman's intuition, eh Darcy?'

'Nothing so fanciful, I assure you, Sir James. Miss Bennet followed a most robust and meticulous methodology.'

'It was no more than a simple exercise in observation and logical deduction based on the known facts,' replied Elizabeth, and she smiled at Darcy. 'I should say it was elementary, Sir John.'

Epilogue

Human nature is such that remorse more frequently accompanies the punishment than the crime itself, but even so, Mrs Bennet shed not a single tear of regret once captured. The days of incarceration following her apprehension were lightened by her satisfied reflections that she had succeeded in securing a husband for Elizabeth, and any chance of repentance died when she heard the news of an engagement between Mr Bingley and Jane.

In keeping with the manner in which Mrs Bennet lived her life, her arrest provoked much commotion and gossip. The revelation of her crimes had the whole neighbourhood in uproar and it was a relief for the family to remove to London after the trial for the weddings of Jane and Bingley, and Elizabeth and Darcy. The shadow of their condemned mother hung over the ceremonies and even the immense happiness of the couples did not provoke the gratitude Mrs Bennet imagined she was owed for her efforts.

After the wedding, Mr Bennet and his two younger daughters returned to Longbourn and found that they could bear the solitude of an outcast family quite well. Their society was far more confined, but a greater freedom was enjoyed in their home. Mr Bennet expanded his library as he had always wished to; Mary spent many a day absorbing improving homilies so that she might recall a virtuous quotation to fit any situation; and Kitty took much delight in slouching, speaking without being reprimanded for her stammer, and partaking of as much cake and sugary tea as she liked without a mother present to object to the deleterious effects on her figure or complexion.

By the following Michaelmas Mr Price, the vicar whose beloved niece and ward Fanny had been one of Mrs Bennet's victims, called upon the family. After much consultation with his conscience, and more still with Sir John Middleton, he felt that it was his Christian duty to offer the olive branch of public forgiveness to the Bennets. An invitation to Hartfield from Mr Woodhouse soon followed. After that the neighbourhood's hostility to the Bennet family thawed. While the tragic scandal of Mrs Bennet's crimes had left a deep scar on the community, her soon-to-be widower and motherless children could not be spurned and held to blame forever.

Mrs Bennet, right unto the very end, felt little remorse over the whole ordeal – or rather she saw no reason to reproach herself for her actions – but she did permit herself to lament that she had been caught. That she was barred from organising and executing not one, but two of her daughters' weddings was a hardship for the family that she felt most grievously.

Still, she had the comfort of knowing that her ingenuity alone was responsible for her two eldest daughters finding husbands. If she had not murdered all those girls, then Darcy and Bingley would have never come and never fallen in love with Elizabeth and Jane. How could she reproach herself for her actions when such fine matches had been obtained?

She likewise took comfort in the knowledge that dear little Lydia had been sent to live with a cousin of Mr Bennet. The Devon branch of the Bennet line occupied a fine old house rather grandly situated upon the moors, and Mrs Bennet felt quite content imagining her darling pug scampering upon the misty heath and grasslands. Lydia had such a handsome face and charming disposition that Mrs Bennet was assured she would quite make her mark upon Devon society.

It was with thoughts such as these that Mrs Bennet ended her days. While so many others approach the gallows with a heavy heart burdened with regret and shame, Mrs Bennet smiled even as the noose was dropped around her neck. With two daughters married to two such fine gentlemen, she should have thought herself a very poor mother indeed if she could not rejoice in such a fortunate and happy ending.

Fin.

Made in United States
North Haven, CT
09 November 2022